DELUSIONAL LOVE

BY

SAGE YOUNG

DELUSIONAL LOVE

Published by Sage Young (Author)
www.authorsageyoung.com

Edited by Sage Young

Formatted by Sage Young

Cover Design: David B. Eggleston & Sage Young
Copyright © 2013 Sage Young
All rights reserved.

ISBN-13: 978-1493596669
ISBN-10: 1493596667

DEDICATION

This book is dedicated to all my friends and family. Thank you all. A special thank you to my significant other David, you are my rock.

ACKNOWLEDGMENTS

I'd like to acknowledge my family members and special friends who gave endless support and multiple reads. You helped to make my dream a reality.   I love you. Thank you so very much for your enthusiasm for my writing. Your exceptional feedback and editing skills have been invaluable.

SAGE YOUNG

TABLE OF CONTENTS

CHAPTER ONE

THURSDAY, JUNE 9th

Ivan and Ashley bolted through the elevator doors leading into his condominium. He stumbled as he tried to get his footing. Her legs had been wrapped around his waist since they entered the private elevator of his building. There were never any delusions about what Ashley wanted when they were together.

He balanced their weight as his left arm secured her back while his right hand was at the nap of her neck, pulling her closer into the feverous kiss. He slammed her back against the wall in the foyer, bracing her body as he continued the assault on her lips. Moving his hand downward, he began to squeeze her right breast. He preferred the softness of natural breast, not ones enhanced, but she would definitely do for tonight because he really needed to get laid.

The sexy strapless black dress she wore that evening made him the envy of every man in the restaurant. Now it was just a piece of material gathered at her midsection fully exposing her breasts and her black lace thong. He ripped his lips from hers, biting her lower lip as he moved his mouth to her left breast. Her pink nipples were fully erect. He bit her nipple followed by a swipe of his tongue to soothe the sting. She moaned in both pain and pleasure, she loved every minute of it, especially when he was rough.

With her arms wrapped around his neck she positioned her body lower so she could feel his hardness pressed against her heat. She started grinding on him to soothe her aching pussy. She needed him inside her. As he continued to brace her against the wall he moved his hand from her breast to her mound. He could feel her wetness soaking through the lace thong. She gasped as he ripped them away from her body, allowing him full access to her pussy. She started to breathe heavily. He used his thumb to rub her swollen clit as he plunged his middle finger into her heat. She moaned loudly while grinding into his finger.

With every stroke of his thumb her breathing became shallow; she inhaled deeply trying to pull air into her lungs. He inserted another finger and was now using both of them to finger fuck her. His fingers were moving so fast that she fought to match each thrust with her hips. He was the only man who could make her cum using his fingers.

"Ohh..., yes baby, Ohh... Sh."
Before she could utter another word her body shook violently as the pleasure of the orgasm slammed into her. He held her securely as tremors washed through her body.

"Damn baby that felt so good."
She cooed as she lowered her shaky legs to stand upright. She started undoing the belt and zipper on his pants. She lowered herself to her knees as his pants pooled at his feet. She licked her lips slowly while she pulled down his black boxer briefs allowing his manhood to spring free. He kicked his clothing to the side as she inhaled his manly scent. She loved his smell and the massive size of his dick, so long and thick.

Some women would be intimidated by his size, not her; she loved every inch of it. She wrapped her manicured fingers around him, licking the pre cum that glistened at the tip of the head. She wrapped her lips around his cock and took inch after delicious inch into her mouth. He threw his head back and moaned loudly. She looked up at him and smiled, she loved the effect she had on him. *'She was definitely one of the best at giving head'* he thought. She tried to take all of him in her mouth, remembering to relax her throat muscles to reduce the gag factor.

"Shit," he moaned.

He was close to coming in her mouth, growling as she moved him in and out of her warm wet mouth while moving her hand in a circular motion at the base of his dick. She used her other hand to caress his balls. She loved pleasing him. She knew he was close to coming; she started sucking harder wanting him to cum in her mouth. Before he could cum, he yanked her to her feet and carried her to the sofa, then climbed on top of her; he needed to be inside her now, positioning himself at her entrance, when a moment of clarity kicked in.

"Fuck, I need a condom!"

"It's all right baby, I told you, I'm on the pill."

"Arhhhh."He growled as he picked her up and carried her to the bedroom. He placed her on the bed; she quickly removed her dress as he removed the rest of his clothing. He reached into the nightstand and retrieved a condom. The one thing he would never do is rely on a woman to be truthful about birth control; he had too much to lose.

11

He sheathed himself with the condom and climbed on the bed, positioning himself between her legs. He looked into her blue eyes as she stared back at him.

"Wrap your legs around my waist."

His voice commanded and she complied. Without warning he slammed his dick inside her with such force that it took her breath away. Stilling himself, he continued to stare into her eyes waiting for her cue to continue. She smiled as she grabbed his shoulders and tilted her hips forward, she was ready. He withdrew and slammed into her again; her pussy was so wet that his dick glided in and out of her with ease. Thrust after thrust she cried out in both pain and pleasure as she could feel the onset of another orgasm. He knew she was close, he could feel her pulsating around him.

"Yes...... Yes, I'm coming ...."

The spasms shot through her body, before she could catch her breath, he pulled out and she instantly felt the loss.

"Turn over and get on your knees."

She again complied with his command. He knelt behind her grabbing her waist as he pulled her back into his erection. His dick slammed into her, filling her completely. She screamed as the pleasure overrode the pain.

"Yes, fuck me, fuck me," She yelled.

He was only too willing to comply. The frenzied pace caused her to become dizzy. She felt like she was having an out-of-body experience as she tried to keep up with the pace.

"Come for me baby."

He said in a husky but sultry voice. His voice was her undoing. She cried out, as her body was unprepared for the orgasm it was withstanding. Her body was trembling and she felt like she was floating. He sped up his pace as he could feel his release. He continued his onslaught until he spilled his seed into the condom. He followed with a few short thrust and felt her body go limp. He released her and both of their bodies collapsed on the bed.

The sounds of their heavy breathing filled the room as they tried to get their breathing under control. After a few minutes of silence, he rolled over, and looked down at the used condom, *'I'm glad I didn't let my dick overrule my head.'* was his only thought as he grabbed tissues from the nightstand, removed the condom and disposed of it in the wastebasket next to the bed. He turned over to face her; she was already staring at him.

"You can have Danny take you home." He said dismissively. She looked at him and tried not to show the hurt in her face. She loved him and if he allowed himself, she knew he could love her too.

"Huhh? I...I thought you told him you would not need him for the rest of the evening." she said.

"Shit."

He said. He was angry with himself because he really wanted to be alone now. "I did tell him that, oh well I guess you are staying. I need to get some sleep." He turned over not wanting to face her, he really preferred sleeping alone. He pulled the covers up to his waist and tried to sleep. She laid there looking up at the ceiling making sure there was enough space between them because she knew he did not cuddle or spoon, truth be told he did not like to be touched after sex. A smile slowly spread across her face. 'Soon, Ivan, soon you will be mine.' She turned her back to him and dozed off with the thought of becoming Mrs. Ivan Quinn.

Ivan Quinn stood in front of the floor-to-ceiling window, overlooking the City of Brotherly Love in his sprawling condominium, still damp from his shower watching the sunrise. He turned to look at the figure in his bed. Ashley started stirring under the sheets. He wondered how long he could continue with this "arrangement". Lately she was becoming possessive, wanting more of his time, which he had no desire to give. From the start, she knew the deal. He was not interested in a relationship, just the noncommittal arrangement.

Ashley Ross was twenty-seven years old and all things beautiful; at five feet eight inches tall she could go up against any model on the runway in Milan. Her long blonde hair cascaded down her back against her porcelain skin as her body shifted to face him. The color of her eyes was the deepest blue he had ever seen. He turned away from Ashley, refocusing his attention to the city's skyline. He realized that while she was beautiful there was no real chemistry between them. The only thing they shared was great sex and convenience.

She made herself available when he needed a date for the numerous events he attended. He did not want the headache of unwanted attention from women looking for a wealthy husband and a financial benefactor. In turn, Ashley definitely benefited financially. Not only did he pay for her condo and car, he also gave her access to credit cards. It was an unspoken rule that she could purchase an expensive piece of jewelry every time she had to attend a function with him. He did not want or need the complication of a real relationship.

Ivan thought back to the day they met. It was at a fundraiser hosted by the museum where she was the curator. Ivan was speaking with a few business colleagues when Ashley approached him. She introduced herself and asked him if he wanted a tour and they ended up having sex on the desk in her office. That was almost a year ago. And although the sex had been great he didn't want 'this' anymore. He liked Ashley, but he needed to end their arrangement.

Ashley woke up staring at Ivan with lust in her eyes; she was always ready to give herself willingly. She knew Ivan's morning routine. He got up every day at five o'clock, worked out and then showered. She got up while he worked out brushed her teeth and freshened up before he returned to the room, just in case she needed
to please her man before he went into the office. 'A girl could get used to this, waking up in his bed every day' she thought. Only on rare occasions did she actually stay

overnight at his place. Normally, he would go to her condo for sex and leave before sunrise. Or, she would come to his place and when they were done he would have his driver take her home.

As she looked at his obviously freshly showered body she was in awe of him. At 34 years old he was a perfect specimen of a man. He was Italian and Irish and at six foot five inches he was her bronze God. His chest was chiseled with an amazing six-pack stomach and a tight muscular ass that made her wet just thinking about him. She looked over at him and thought *'Soon he will be mine; I can see it in his eyes. I knew he wouldn't be able to resist for long. I only agreed to that fucked up agreement because I knew I would be able to break through that stone exterior and make him mine. Hell, he is one of the richest men in Pennsylvania and one of Philadelphia's most eligible bachelors. Damn, I love him so much.'*

Looking over at the nightstand she smiled as she opened the drawer and retrieved a condom. *'Still a half a box left, we will have to take care of that.'*

"Hey, why don't you come back to bed and continue where we left off at last night."

"I can't, I have to prepare for a meeting this morning. I have another new temp assistant and she is as bad as the last one they sent. God, I miss Bridget, she would prepare for these meetings with her eyes closed and now I can't seem to find someone competent enough to figure out how to put the reports together, let alone do the research needed and make the necessary revisions." It had been six months since Bridget got married and moved to Montana.

He really missed his friend. She was like the little sister he never had. Bridget started with the company shortly after he and his brother started it. She was definitely one of the main cogs that kept the company running. Although he missed her, he was happy that she found someone she loved and who truly loved her. She was a beautiful person inside and out.

Ashley sat back on the bed positioning herself against the headboard. Ashley also thought about Bridget.
'That man-stealing bitch he called an assistant. I could tell from the first time I met her that she was trying to get with Ivan. All those late nights they were supposedly working. Well good riddance; I hope she stays in Montana. It was so easy to get rid of Ms. Perfect. I only needed to find someone to marry her and keep her away from my man.'

Ashley was really proud of her handiwork. *'It actually wasn't that difficult. After signing up for a dating service and letting the prospects know that I was in a newly committed relationship but had a friend who was looking for someone special, but did not like dating services. Luckily she was very attractive and it was really easy to steer dates her way. I would tell them to go by the office pretending to be a vendor and if they liked the way she looked, they should ask her out. Luckily it only took four tries before she was totally taken with one of the men. Men can be so gullible.'* She smiled to herself and thought she could be a matchmaker. *'It did get a little hairy when Bridget's new love felt the need to be totally honest with her and told her about the dating service and my involvement. I told her that I had forgotten about the dating service after Ivan and I started seeing each other. I told her when I saw how handsome he was I immediately thought of her, but I knew if she thought I was involved, she would not give him a chance. Bridget believed every word of it. Damn I'm good.'*

Ashley redirected her attention to Ivan as she watched him go into his walk-in closet.

"You sure baby? I will definitely make it worth your while."

She smiled and set up on her knees letting the sheet fall to the bed to give a clear view of her perky and expensive "D" cup breast. He looked over at the bed as he exited the closet.

"I'll have to take a rain check. Now please get dressed I need to leave soon."

Ivan wanted her dressed and out of his house. He really needed to end this arrangement with Ashley but he would wait until after the completion of the major acquisition he was working on.

Ivan stormed out of his office walking over to the desk where his current assistant sat, this was the final straw for him. Not only did she not complete the research needed for today's meeting, but she made revisions to the wrong report.

"What.The.Fuck.Is.This?"

He labored over each word as he threw documents on the desk. She jumped, almost leaping out the rolling desk chair she was sitting in. Ivan continued barely above a whisper, but clearly furious.

"All you had to do was verify the items I outlined make the revisions, and get the necessary copies made. Was that too difficult? It's not brain surgery. Hell, the Internet does the GOD DAMN verifications for you."

Tears began to spill over from the young woman's eyes as she quickly gathered her belongings.

"I cannot work under these conditions. I'm sorry Mr. Quinn, I will notify the agency to send someone else."

She said with a shaky, soft voice. Ignoring the exiting crying woman he retreated to his office to call human resources.

"I don't care who you have to kill, just get me someone who can walk and talk at the same time!"

He slammed down the phone as Adam Quinn, his younger brother walked in. He was just as handsome as Ivan, with the same amazing sea green eyes 32 years old, chiseled body not overly muscular, but it was evident that he worked out. At six foot three inches he was a little shorter than his big brother, but was equally as breath taking. Ivan darted his eyes at his brother.

"Hey bro, I just saw your newest assistant running by me crying. At this rate you will run through every employee at every temp agency in town before the
month is over."

"Very funny, we have a meeting in two hours and our reports are fucked up, so now that you are here you can help me put these reports together before we meet with the rest of the committee." Ivan buzzed his secretary, Betty Connors.

"Betty come into my office I need your assistance on this project."

After the meeting Ivan had a message on his desk informing him that a new temp would be there on Monday morning.

CHAPTER TWO

FRIDAY, JUNE 10th

"Steph, you are a lifesaver, I am so glad you are available."

Stephanie Young stood in the office of Brianna Robinson, her best friend since elementary school. Stephanie was a strikingly beautiful woman with hazel colored eyes and caramel colored skin. At five feet seven inches everything she wore seemed to fit her like a glove. Standing there in a gold colored sleeveless blouse and pencil skirt she looked every bit of the corporate image. Stephanie looked at Brianna. *'My best friend is a natural beauty and I wish I could get her to see herself as everyone else does.'*

Brianna was five feet six inches with cocoa colored skin and a beautiful head of wild curly hair. Brianna never had to wear makeup because her skin was impeccable. Her daily make up regiment consisted of eyeliner and lip-gloss. Her slender figure was something that she always had to work on and she was diligent about keeping her body in shape, but you would never know by the clothes she wore to hide her figure.

Brianna always wore the latest fashion, but nothing too tight or too short. Although she was very beautiful, she was extremely shy and did not socialize outside of work other than their monthly girl's night out. Stephanie remembered when they were back in elementary school; Brianna would always sit by herself reading and Stephanie would sit beside Brianna at lunch, trying to talk to her, but Brianna was not very talkative, always giving one-word answers or just nodding. After a while they became fast friends and inseparable to this day.

"Okay Bri, what does the job entail and why are you so desperate to fill the position?" Stephanie growled. "Stop being so negative, this position is right up your alley, now that you have completed real estate school."

Stephanie was previously a paralegal working at a major law firm in Center City Philadelphia until she was laid off along with 100 other employees when the firm decided to downsize. With the economy being what it was, she was not able to find another job right away, so she decided to follow one of her many dreams and go to Real Estate School. Stephanie completed the program and was again looking for employment. She had many aspirations that she had not yet accomplished. *'Dreams Deferred'* was how Stephanie referred to them.

"First let me just say thank you for agreeing to fill the position. I think they are looking for someone who is available for six months. It's with a major acquisitions firm that deals primarily in real estate. I think it would be a wonderful opportunity for you." Brianna said confidently. 'And we can't keep anyone in that position for longer than two weeks. The last one didn't last two days.'

"Bri, stop talking to me like I'm one of your employees in need of one of your pep talks because you know I'm allergic to bullshit. Tell me straight up without the ass kissing. What's up with this position you obviously can't fill with any of your employees?"

"Alright, alright, I'm going to give it to you straight."

Brianna said exasperated. "This client is very difficult to work for, and by difficult I mean, he is an asshole. I can't keep anyone in that position longer than it takes to complete the paperwork for this position." Brianna said frustrated.

"So when in doubt, throw your best friend under the bus." Stephanie replied.

"No, it's not like that and you know it. You are the most assertive, strong-willed, no-nonsense person I know." Brianna said.

"By assertive, strong-willed no-nonsense you mean pushy, opinionated, and kick ass first and take names later type of person."

"Well, yeah. Look this client is threatening to pull my contract and go with another temp agency if I can't get a competent person with a backbone. I really need your help and I'm calling in one of my favors." Stephanie flopped in the closest chair next to her.

"Are you sure about this Bri, you know me, I can't promise I won't tell this clown where to go if he disrespects me." Stephanie said.

"Well, I'll tell you this;; if he can't work with you then they can pull my contract because I'm out of options."

"Alright, alright but this has to count for two favors." Stephanie said defeated.

Brianna jumped out of her chair and ran up to her best friend and hugged her.

"Thank you, thank you, thank you."

"Don't thank me yet, we will see after I start on Monday."

Brianna and Stephanie sat and discussed the particulars of the position and what was expected. After Stephanie completed the necessary paper work to become an official employee of the Robinson Employment Agency, Brianna handed the paperwork to her assistant for processing.

"Make sure you put a rush on this paper work, I don't want any delays in having Ms. Young start work on Monday."

They headed out the door to meet their other best friend Tara for happy hour at Club Pulsate, one of the hottest nightclubs in Philly. Twenty minutes later Brianna and Stephanie were walking in the door.

"Why did we have to come here? Why couldn't we just go out to dinner and enjoy a nice meal?" Brianna complained.

"Because Bri, it was Ty's turn to choose and she wanted to come here, now stop complaining, loosen a couple of the buttons on that blouse and relax."

They both immediately began to look around the club for Tara. Tara Steward was the most outgoing of the trio. She had a tight body and was not afraid to show it. Her friends often teased her about having come from Cherokee heritage because she had naturally straight black hair that came down her back, deep brown eyes, and chocolate skin that looked smooth as silk. At five feet five, Tara was the shortest of the group, but you would never know it because she always wore at least four-inch heels.

Tara commanded attention when she walked into a room. She walked with such confidence that most men and women took notice when she entered. They spotted Tara on the dance floor she waved and made a pointing gesture to indicate their table. They took a seat, ordered drinks and prepared themselves for what the evening would bring. Tara finally came off the dance floor and they ordered another round of drinks.

Lawrence Peirce and Adam Quinn walked into Club Pulsate with clients who were from out of town and looking to have some fun while visiting Philadelphia.

"You owe me big for this." Lawrence whispered to Adam.

"Whatever man, after all the shit I've gotten you out of, you owe me this and your first born." Adam jokingly said to Lawrence.

Lawrence thought back to their college days. Adam was right; he had gotten him out of quite a few jams. Adam and Lawrence were roommates all four years at Brown University. Lawrence was known for having a temper when pushed too far, he considered himself a person that could not tolerate bullshit. He never had a problem with telling people where to go when he felt like they were trying to get over on him. On more than one occasion Adam had to be the peacemaker when he got into it with motherfuckas who tried to challenge him. It wasn't easy being an African American male, attending a predominately white prestigious Ivy League University. Lawrence felt like he was being challenged at every turn, but Adam was different.

He was a cool ass white boy and their friendship was almost immediate. When they graduated, Lawrence attended law school at Temple University and Adam joined his brother at his Real Estate Investment firm. Lawrence specialized in Real Estate law and was hired by Quinn Investments right out of law school and had been there ever since. Now tonight, he allowed Adam to talk him into hanging out with dudes that looked like they were ready to get into some trouble.

The two young investors were from Ohio, interested in acquiring property in the area. After the business deals were done they wanted a taste of Philly's nightlife. Both Adam and Lawrence were familiar with this club, as they were VIP members; the employees were familiar with them and catered to their needs. Upon entering the club, they were immediately ushered to a private booth that gave them the perfect view of the club and its patrons. They ordered a bottle of Patron Platinum Tequila, after the second round of shots their clients headed down to mingle in the club.

"Hey man, you have one hour then I'm out." Lawrence stated.

"Look! Isn't that Brianna Robinson?"

Lawrence looked around confused, not really knowing whom he was talking about.

"You know, we use her temp agency." Adam said without waiting for a response as he headed toward her table.

"Hey, it's Brianna right? Brianna Robinson."

"Well, hello Mr. Quinn, it's nice seeing you again."

"Likewise, are you here by yourself" Adam said already knowing the answer because he could see two other drinks and purses.

"No I'm the designated drink and purse watcher; my friends are on the dance floor." She said with a smile. Adam took the seat next to Brianna.

"So, do you come here often?" He regretted the words as they fell out of his mouth; it was the oldest pick up line. She raised an eyebrow as if she was thinking the same thing.

"No, I am not a club person, but it was not my choice this month." Brianna said a little annoyed. Adam looked at her confused.

"I don't understand."

"Well, my friends and I do a monthly girls night out and we take turns choosing what we will do."

"So I'm guessing it wasn't your month to choose."
She shook her head as her friends were heading to the table.

"Can you guess which one of my friends chose this month?" She whispered to Adam.
As Stephanie and Tara approached to table, they were both eyeing Adam. While Stephanie walked Tara chose to dance all the way back to the table telling her friends.
"I love this place, they have the best music and the finest men in Philly. Speaking of which, who's your friend, Bri?"

"Stephanie and Tara this is Adam Quinn; Adam, this is Stephanie Young and Tara Steward."

"Nice to meet you ladies. Look, my friend and I have a private booth if you would like to join us." Before Brianna could decline the offer, Tara spoke up.

"We would love to, give us a minute and we will meet you at your booth."

Adam whispered in Brianna's ear. "My guess would be Tara." Brianna smiled.

"What was that about?" Stephanie asked as he walked away.

"Yeah, don't hold out. What did he say?" Tara chimed in.

"It was nothing and I wish you had asked before agreeing to join them. You know I don't mix my business life with my social life."

"Who are you kidding, Bri you don't have a social life." Tara said.

"How do you know him, is he one of your clients?" Stephanie asked.

"Yes, he is actually going to be one of your bosses come Monday."

"Oh hell no, I am not socializing with them. It's time to go Ty"

"Well, we already agreed so let's just have one drink and we can leave." Tara pleaded. They agreed and walked to the booth.

"No Adam, I am not feeling this. I told you I would give you one hour with these clowns and my hour is up. It's time for me to go."

Lawrence said determined to leave.

"Wait until you see the ladies that are coming. I bet you will change your mind"

"Yeah right!" Lawrence said with a smirk.

"Just one drink. If you don't like the company then I will make an excuse for you to leave." Adam pleaded.

"Okay. One, Dri..." Before Lawrence could finish his statement the three beauties walking his way mesmerized him, all Sistas.

"Dammmn!! They are all fine. So how do you know them?" Before Adam could respond they approached the table.

"Who in the world is that fine chocolate drop sitting next to your friend Bri?" Tara whispered.

"Guess we are about to find out." Brianna said approaching the table.

They made introductions and settled into lighthearted conversations, they talked about their careers, what colleges they attended and good restaurants in Philly. Adam offered his condolences in advance to Stephanie because she was going to be working primarily for his older brother Ivan. Tara and Lawrence were so into each other, they forgot anyone else was at the table. They were in their own private conversation. After several minutes, Adam's clients reappeared. *'Shit, I forgot they were here'* Adam said to himself.

"Who are the lovely ladies?" One of the clients said with lustful look in his eyes. Lawrence immediately got an attitude, *'If they say one disrespectful word, I'm going to drop their asses,'* he thought to himself as he eyed Adam with a disgusted look on his face. Adam looked over at Lawrence and could read his body language; he was feeling the same way. They did another round of introductions and one of the clients sat a little too close to Brianna.

"So what do you do for fun?" He whispered in Brianna's ear.

"OOOOKAY, it's time to go." Brianna said as she stood.

"Why are you leaving so soon Brianna?" Adam asked as he shot a dirty look to his client.

"Did he say something to offend you?" He whispered in her ear.

She felt his warm breath on her neck and the tingly feeling she felt surprised her.

"No...No I'm just tired and I uh...stayed longer than I intended too," she whispered back to him.

His smell permeated her nostrils giving her a warm feeling inside, she wanted to bury her face in his chest and inhale deeply. She closed her eyes momentary to get her senses together. As she opened her eyes and turned to look at him their faces were so close she thought he was going to kiss her. She quickly turned to face the rest of the group.

"Enjoy the rest of your evening everyone." She said trying to hide her flustered look. Everyone else stood as Brianna made her way out of the booth.

"Let me walk you to the door." Adam said to Brianna not ready to end their time together.

"No, stay I will be fine." Brianna said softly.
"I am heading out too, I have to get up early tomorrow. What about you Ty?" Stephanie said.

"Huh, oh I'm going to hang out here for a little bit longer." She said looking over at Lawrence.

"I will make sure she gets home safely." Lawrence said not taking his eyes off of Tara.

"Will do." Tara responded.

"I guess that leaves just us." Adam said to the clients. "What do you guys want to do next?"

Lawrence pulled in front of Tara's townhome.

"Do you want to come in for a drink?" Tara said in a hushed tone.

"That may be a dangerous proposition Ty." Lawrence said confidently.
"I'll take my chances." She said smiling.

They walked through the door into the living room. Her living room was decorated with mostly African art; the colors were soft browns with a hint of orange. The atmosphere of her home gave Lawrence a warm feeling.

"Have a seat;; I'll be back in a sec."

Tara went to the kitchen and came back with a bottle of wine and two wine glasses. She sat down next to Lawrence on the sofa, he looked at her and before anything could be said he lowered his lips down onto hers. She moaned into his mouth as he pulled her into his lap. She pulled her mouth away, looking into his brown eyes, as she straddled him allowing her short skirt to hike up above her thighs.

"Damn, you are so beautiful Tara."

She leaned into him pressing her lips against his, parting her lips to receive his tongue. As the kiss deepened their tongues mingled together. Tara could feel his manhood growing against her lace thong. *'Girl slow this down before it's too late'* she thought. *'Huh, who am I kidding, it's already too late,'* she couldn't or wouldn't stop. She was really feeling him. He was fine and his smell was so intoxicating. She could feel the heat building between her thighs.

Lawrence grabbed the hem of her blouse and pulled it over her head revealing her black lace bra. He unsnapped her bra releasing her small perky breast. Tara leaned back as Lawrence took the left breast in his mouth while massaging the right one. He loved the feel of her breast, he alternated putting the right one in his mouth while massaging the left.

"Tara, I want you so bad, but I don't want you to do something you're not comfortable with." He whispered in her ear. The heat from his breath was sending her hormones into overdrive.

"Oh, I'm more than comfortable." She said as she started grinding her hips into his groin. He moaned and his lips came crashing down onto hers, kissing her so thoroughly she could not get her breath. She reached down, unzipped his pants and released his manhood. She smiled with delight, *'Okay Mr. Lawrence, I see you are packing' more than enough equipment,'* she thought as she continued to grind against him. He moaned loudly as she feverously sucked on his tongue as she unbuttoned his shirt. His chest was hard and muscular. She ran her fingers gently down his six-pack down to his pants. He pulled back allowing them to catch their breath and halting her progress.

"Girl, you are going to kill me." He said and stared at her with hooded eyes.

"Stand up!" He commanded. His husky voice sent shivers through her body. She stood up and he quickly removed his pants and boxers. His manhood was hard and erect. Tara eyes widened as she took note of his size. A devilish smile crept onto her face as he sat back on the sofa, pulling her closer to him as she stood in front of him.

He unzipped her skirt and pulled it down her leg, letting it pool at her feet. He put his face in between her legs, his nose laid against her thong and he took a deep breath.

"God you smell so good."

He said against her pussy. The vibration from his voice sent tingling feelings throughout her body. He hooked his finger into her thong and pulled it down her legs. She stepped out of the clothes and pushed them to the side. She stood there in front of him naked and unashamed. He wanted her so bad his dick hurt. He ran his tongue along

the outside lips of her clean-shaven fold. He pulled her left leg over his shoulder as he inserted his finger inside her. Tara moaned as she put her hands
on his shoulders to brace herself. She was so wet. He lowered his head to lick her juices. He removed his finger and inserted his tongue moving it in and out of her.

"Oh my God it feels so fucking good. Don't stop. Oh my God, I'm coming, I'm cu………."

He could feel her body trembling as her juices ran down his tongue. He grabbed her waist to steady her so she would not fall. Lawrence continued to suck her juices until she was almost dry. He reached in his pants pocket for a condom and sheathed himself.

"Come here."

He grabbed her waist, bringing her into the straddled position. "You look so beautiful when you cum." He rubbed the head of his dick at her entrance and pulled her onto him, filling her completely. Lawrence stayed completely still, giving her body a chance to adjust to his size. She tilted her body and leaned in to take him in further. She lifted her body off of his and slammed back down onto him. He almost came when he felt shockwaves going through his body. He steadied her waist and smiled at her.

"Slow down babe, I don't want this party to be over before it gets started."

He took a deep breath, he really needing to concentrate. He grabbed both of her breasts, as she started moving slowly up and down his thick rod. Her chocolate drop nipples were erect. He swiped her nipple with his tongue before placing the entire nipple in his mouth and began to suck. He moved to the side of her breast; sucking so hard he was leaving marks in his path.

"God you are so thick" she purred as she moved faster.

He grabbed her waist thrusting upwards to meet her pounding. "OH fuck!" She said breathing heavily. "You are so wet and tight." He said as he tried to control the speed. She couldn't take it anymore she put her hands on his shoulders, lifting herself almost all the way off of him and then came down on him hard.

"Shit girl, you are going to kill me."

He said as he continued to thrust upward meeting her stroke for stroke. They moved so hard and fast, they were both having a hard time catching their breath. He pulled her off of him and placed her on the sofa. He climbed between her legs, grabbing each leg with his arms, he raised her legs to the height of his chest and slammed his dick into her. She screamed with pleasure.

"Ohh shit. Yes, baby, I'm coming again, you feel so good...."

He could feel her body jerk and start to tremble; he continued to pound into her. He felt like a man possessed he could not get enough. He felt her pulsating around him, milking him, his body stiffened as he came so hard he felt dizzy. That was by far the hardest he'd ever cum, he collapsed on top of her. They lay there while their heart rates adjusted and breathing slowed down. He looked into her eyes as his lips connected with hers, devouring hers with such a hunger she could not think straight; he pulled his mouth away.

"Where's the bedroom?" He whispered in her ear and she led him upstairs.

Lawrence left at 6 o'clock the next morning, he would have stayed longer but he needed to get into the office to finish working on a legal brief. Tara was so tired but she put on her robe and walked him to the door. He kissed her goodbye with the promise of calling her later. She closed and locked the door and decided to take a shower, just as she walked towards the stairs the doorbell rang. *'I wonder if Lawrence forgot something.'*

She swung the door open, "Did you forget something or just miss..... What are you doing here?" She said shocked and a little frightened to see the man standing in front of her.

"You don't seem excited to see your fiancé?" He said with a smug look on his face.

CHAPTER THREE

MONDAY, JUNE 13th

Monday morning came around too quickly for Stephanie. She grabbed her travel coffee mug and was out the door. She wanted to be early to get the lay of the land at her new job. Stephanie entered the high-rise building and made her way to the 40th floor. The receptionist announced her arrival. Ivan's secretary came out to meet her.

"Hi my name is Betty Connors, I'm Mr. Quinn's secretary. You are really early."

"I know, I just wanted to settle in before getting started." Stephanie said.

"Okay, I will show you where you sit and when you are ready I can go over your assignments."

Betty introduced her to the rest of the staff and escorted her to where she would sit. Betty's desk was in the common area. The door directly behind Betty's desk led to Stephanie's desk, which was situated in a small office right outside of Ivan Quinn's office, which meant he would have to walk through her area to get to his office.
'Great, this is an interesting setup.' She thought. Betty made sure her office was fully stocked with all the supplies she would need.

After thoroughly reviewing the assignments left by Mr. Quinn, Stephanie got to work. She was so engrossed in her work she did not realize that it was almost noon. Betty walked in and asked her if she needed anything before she went to lunch.

"I do have a few questions regarding the reports I'm expected to complete." Stephanie said.

"Well, I know that Mr. Quinn will be here sometime this afternoon but if you are really pressed for information you can call Mr. Quinn's previous assistant, Bridget Wolf, no wait, Swain. She is newly married. Her number is in your contacts list."

"No, that's okay, if she doesn't work here anymore I don't want to contact her."

"Oh sweetie, it's okay, she and Mr. Quinn were very close and I have called her on several occasions when Mr. Quinn was being, huh, let's just say, difficult. She worked for him for several years and knows how to deal with him better than anyone I've ever seen."

Those were Betty's parting words as she went to lunch. Stephanie sat at her desk and thought about it. "What the hell, I guess it can't hurt." She picked up the phone and after a long conversation with Bridget, Stephanie was feeling better about completing her assignments. She got to work and after completing all the assignments, she pulled out the sandwich she bought for lunch.

Bridget told her where to locate a file that would give her all the background information on the company, giving her a better understanding of who she was working for. She got up to return the file to the filing cabinet when the file slipped out of her hand and papers scattered all on the floor. As she bent over to retrieve the papers, Mr. Ivan Quinn walked in.

As Ivan rounded Betty's empty desk, he retrieved his messages from his message bin. He entered the inner office, looked over to see if the new assistant was there and saw a very curvaceous bottom half of a woman bent over, picking up scattered papers. He cleared his throat, which caused Stephanie to quickly spin around still bent over. Ivan's first look into the face of this woman caused his breath to hitch. She was breathtakingly beautiful with the most striking hazel eyes. Her skin was the color of caramel, smooth and flawless. Stephanie stood upright and he was able to take in the entire package. She wasn't a skinny woman, but had one of the most curvaceous bodies he had ever seen attached to an amazing set of legs.

"Hi. May I help you?" Stephanie asked. She was a little taken back by the gorgeous man that stood in front of her, even through the suit, she could see he had a muscular frame. He had a squared off chin and piercing green eyes that seem to glow. She felt her body tingle as she looked into his amazing eyes.

"Yes, you can help me by showing me where you are with the assignment I left for you to complete." He turned away without another word and headed into his office closing the door behind him. *'Okay, fantasy is over. That went well.*

The first time I see my new boss, he gets a clear view of my ass.'

Ivan stared out the window as he tried to get his breathing under control. Never in his entire life had the sight of a woman affected him that way and he had been around some of the most beautiful women in the world. Hell, he bedded some of the most beautiful women in the world. So why was this woman affecting him like he was some goddamn teenager with his first crush. He sat at his desk and took a deep breath and waited for his new assistant to enter.

Stephanie gathered her assignments as she thought about her first interaction with her new boss. *'This is going to be interesting. He did not even introduce himself. I didn't expect him to be warm and fuzzy, but he could have at least introduced himself "Hi I'm Ivan Quinn and I will be your tormentor for the next several months". Would that have been so difficult?'* She thought as she knocked on his door.

"Come!" Was the only response she received. She entered the office; it was similar in style to the partners at her previous job. It had a beautiful view of the city's skyline.

"Have a seat. You are?" Ivan said.

'That's it, he has one more time to treat me rudely and we are going to have a heart to heart,' Stephanie thought. "My name is Stephanie Young and I was assigned to your firm by Robinson Associates." She handed him her completed assignments and watched as he reviewed her reports. *'Bri is going to owe me big.'* Ivan reviewed the reports fully expecting to have major corrections, because to date, he

had not had a good track record with that agency. His plan was to have human resources look into hiring a new temp agency. He was pleasantly surprised to find that she had done the reports exactly the way he wanted them.

He had to admit that the formatting and style was impressive. He looked up from the reports,

"Okay, you're done for today. There will be assignments placed on your desk in the morning with timelines and expectations." He immediately picked up a folder from his desk and turned his chair towards the window.
'Did he just dismiss me?' Stephanie thought as she tried to control her temper.

"Thank you, uh...Mr. Quinn. And I assume that's who you are considering we were never officially introduced. I just wanted to thank you for this opportunity and ask that since this is my first day *'and hopefully not my last.'* I was hoping I could get some type of feedback, verbal or written so that I know that I am completing the work to your satisfaction, instead of getting a call from the agency telling me not to show up again." She gave him a smile that did not reach her eyes, turned on her heels and walked towards the door "Have a good evening, Mr. Uh, Quinn," Again emphasizing the point that he neglected to introduce himself. A faint smile formed on his face as she shut the door.

"That went well," she said softly and gathered her belongs.

Stephanie walked into her condo, shuffled through her mail and hit the button on the answering machine to retrieve her messages. There were a few from telemarketers and one from Brianna asking her to call when she got home. She was interested in how the day went.

"Oh Bri, I may have blown this for you," she said while tossing her mail in her mail bin. She went to her kitchen poured herself a glass of wine and prepared to take a long soak in tub.

Ivan sat at his desk rereading the same paragraph of the report. He could not get his new assistant out of his mind. *'She's so strictly beautiful. And those eyes! She has the most amazing hazel eyes.'* He could still faintly smell her intoxicatingly soft flowery scent. Still in deep thought, he felt his phone vibrate in his pocket.

"Yes."

"Hey baby, are we meeting for dinner?" Ashley asked. Ivan really did not feel like dealing with her tonight. "No, I have to work late. I will call you tomorrow." "Please Ivan, I really need to discuss something with you," she pleaded. He let out a frustrated sigh. *'I really need to end this.'*

"Okay, I will meet you at Salandros." He said with irritation in his voice.

"Good, I will meet you there at eight o'clock." She squealed. Ashley hung up the phone; her plan was already in motion to get Ivan to marry her. If everything went as planned, she would have a ring really soon. Ashley turned around to face her best friend Samantha Marino.

"I don't know Ash, all this plotting to get a man to marry you will backfire. I think you should be straight with him and tell him directly that you want to move your relationship to the next level with a commitment, but be ready to walk away if he is not willing to commit. You are a beautiful person inside and out and deserve someone who will love you completely and not subject you to some screwed up arrangement that has you at his beck and call."

"I don't want anyone else, I want and will get Ivan." Ashley said slightly irritated with her friend. "I know he loves me and just needs a little push to make him admit it to himself."

"I don't know Ashley. I don't want to see you get hurt like your last relationship and how badly it ended, you were an emotional wreck for months."

"This is different Sam, why can't you just be happy for me; I don't need another one of your lectures."

Ashley loved her best friend but sometimes she could be so judgmental and irritating.

"Well, I have to go home and get ready for my date. I will call you later. Wish me luck." Ashley said as she sashayed out of Samantha's apartment.

"I hope you know what you are doing and good luck". Samantha was really worried about her friend. 'I hope she knows what she's doing. Her last relationship ended so badly that I didn't think she would recover emotionally, but she came through really strong. I really don't want to see her heading down that road again.'

Ashley walked into the restaurant fifteen minutes late. She wanted to make sure Ivan was there so she could make a grand entrance like she always did, but tonight was different so she really needed to blow Ivan away with her appearance. As usual Ashley turned almost every head as she walked through the restaurant. She wore a beautiful red sheath dress with an illusion back and short sleeves lending allure to a square-neck fashioned with horizontal pleats throughout the body for a modern, tiered effect. As she approached the table she noticed Ivan's eyes widen. He stood, held out the seat for her, and kissed her on the cheek.

"You look beautiful as usual." They both sat and the waitress came over to the table.

"Can I get you something to drink?" The waitress looked at Ashley.

"Yes, I will have a glass of white wine." She said without looking at the waitress almost dismissively.

"How about you sir, would you like another gin and tonic?"

"Yes, thank you." He said giving the waitress eye contact with a faint smile. The waitress returned with their drinks and took their order. They settled into small talk until their food arrived. Ashley could tell that Ivan was slightly distracted and she wanted all of his attention.

"I've been thinking Ivan, the Forrester's annual formal event is coming up and I thought, uh, it would be nice if we could do something special after the event to celebrate the fact that our arrangement has lasted over a year, maybe go away for the weekend." *'Please, this has to work'* she thought. Nervously she continued: "We have both been burning the midnight oil at work and I think we could use a break. No strings attached, of course, just relaxation and fun, you won't regret it and I will totally make it worth your while."

He looked at her with a raised eyebrow, but did not answer.

"Don't answer me now, just think about it and let me know."

"Look Ashley, I don't want you to think this arrangement is going somewhere, because it's not. I have been upfront with you from the beginning. You know I am not looking for a relationship. I have too many things going."

Ashley was extremely disappointed but not surprised.
She had done her homework on Mr. Ivan Quinn and she knew that he had not been attached to any woman longer than six months; so she thought she gained the upper hand because they had been seeing each other for almost a year.

"Ashley, I think that it's time we end this. I really need to concentrate on my business with no distractions. You are a great woman but I think this has run its course." Ashley was fuming inside *'Distraction? He thinks I'm a distraction. Well you are not getting off that easy Ivan,'* She thought. *'I hope my plan B is working.'* She thought as she tried to get her anger under control.

"Fine Ivan, we both knew this would end. I was just hoping we'd have more time together. At least go on a commitment-free weekend getaway." She said trying to keep her voice from trembling.

"That's not going to happen, Ashley." Ivan responded in a monotone voice. Ashley wanted to scream; she had to get her anger in check.

"Fine Ivan, at least we can remain friends. Possibly friends with occasional benefits." She said with a smile that did not reach her eyes. Ivan looked at her, thinking how great the sex had been between the two of them and an occasional hook up couldn't hurt.

"Speaking of benefits, will you at least give me tonight to have my way with you?" She said with a slight laugh. "You are definitely a piece of work." He responded with a slight smile.

After dinner they headed to Ivan's condo. As soon as they reached the foyer Ashley immediately pulled Ivan into a passionate kiss. She parted her lips inviting his tongue and he obliged. She kissed him with urgency as she ran her fingers through his hair, pulling him in tighter to the kiss. After a few seconds she released him.

"Why don't you lock up and I will meet you in the bedroom," Ashley said seductively.

"Okay, I just need to make a call," Ivan said.

"Don't take too long," she said with a lustful look in her eyes. Ivan walked to his bar and poured himself a drink, sat down, and dialed the phone.

While waiting for Ivan Ashley went over to Ivan's nightstand to make sure he was still using the same box of condoms she placed there a month ago. *'Damn, we've only used half the box of condoms.'* She thought back on how she had purchased the same brand Ivan uses, carefully poked holes in every one of the condoms in the box and replaced his with her tampered box. She was careful to make sure that she matched the same number as was in the original box. *'This has to work.'* She was confident that she was the only one Ivan was sleeping with; there was no chance he would be using those condoms with anyone else. Ashley quietly closed the drawer. She stripped down to her red lace bra and thong and waited patiently for Ivan.

Ivan hung up the cell phone and his mind instantly thought of his new assistant. 'What the hell is wrong with me?' He thought as he tried to clear his head. Ashley appeared in the room and walked over to him.

"What's taking so long, I almost started without you." She said with a sexy smile.

"I'm coming, I just needed to return some calls."

She walked over to him and straddled his lap. Looking into her eyes he could see the hunger. He gripped both of her breasts as he closed his eyes and brought his lips down on hers. He started envisioning his new assistant and his manhood began to rise. He took her left breast into his mouth sucking on her hard nipple through the lace. She leaned her head back and moaned, began to undo his pants and reached in to release his dick. He grabbed her hands halting her progress.

"Let's go to the bedroom." He said as he lifted her up and carried her to the bedroom. Once inside the bedroom Ivan lowered Ashley onto the bed and began to undress.

"No, let me do that." Ashley said as she unbuttoned his shirt revealing his black undershirt. She quickly removed the undershirt, moaning as she took sight of his amazing muscular form while tracing his rock abs with her fingers. She ran her fingers down his chest, and over his stomach. She lowered herself to her knees, unzipped his pants and pulled down his pants and boxers together. Ivan stepped out of the clothes that pooled at his feet and kicked them to the side. She inhaled deeply, taking in his scent: a combination of woody and musky scent. His smell was intoxicating; she was in awe at the sight of his dick. She took him in her mouth slowly savoring the taste of him as she heard him moan loudly. The sounds of his enjoyment caused her inner thighs to moisten. She tried to take all of him into her mouth holding the base of his dick, turning her hand in a circular motion with every stroke of her lips, creating a suction feeling. She could tell see was pleasing her man by the sounds that were coming from his mouth.

He couldn't take it anymore he needed to fuck her. He growled and lifted her onto the bed, "You have a very talented mouth." He said in a low tone. She smiled as he reached over to grab a condom and quickly sheathed himself moving between her thighs. Ivan lowered his mouth onto her breast as he placed two fingers inside of her. She was always wet for him. She arched her back and moaned. He began to thrust his fingers into her wet warm canal while using his thumb to rub her swollen clit. She moved her hips to meet every stroke.

"Oh baby I'm coming; Yes Ivan. Yes. Oh God, yes."
Ivan felt her body trembling as he thrust one last time. Ivan lay on the bed and pulled Ashley on top of him. "Ride me baby." He said as he placed his dick at her entrance of her fold, she slowly lowered her body down onto his, taking all of him inside her. She began to move faster, riding him as he thrust his body upward. She moved her hips up and down, tilting her body forward with every down thrust. Ivan
moaned, the constant connection of their bodies created an incredible sensation. He pulled her off of him and placed her on the bed. She wrapped her legs around his waist. He thrust into her as she tilted her hips to take him in deeper. Ivan closed his eyes concentrating on the feeling when the face, the beautiful face of Stephanie appeared in his mind. He instantly halted his motion and Ashley knew something was wrong, she started to panic. *Does he somehow know that I tampered with the condoms? Oh God! He is going to freak,'* she thought.

"What's wrong baby?" She asked concerned.

"Nothing's wrong. Just too much on my mind," as he began to move again, "But your body is helping to relieve the stress from my mind and body," he said as he
thrust again hard. He began to pick up the pace, as did his labored breathing. Ashley started to scream as she came again. He could feel her body trembling beneath him has her inner muscles started to pulsate around him. He could

not hold on any longer and with one last hard thrust he came hard. He rolled over and laid on his back until his heart rate slowed to normal. He went into the bathroom to discard the condom and came back to bed.

Ashley understood the deal; he was not the cuddling type, so she pulled the covers on top of her nude body, positioned herself close to Ivan's body and lay on her side facing him as he lay on his back with his arms behind his head. She looked at the beautiful man lying beside her and hoped it worked. She hoped that the pain-staking task of putting holes in every one of those condoms would yield her the results she was looking for. She was currently ovulating and needed this to work. If not this time, hopefully, as long as they remained friends with benefits she still had a chance.

Ivan lay there looking at the ceiling as his thoughts swirled around in his head. He was thinking about his current situation with Ashley, the fact that he couldn't stop Stephanie from invading his thoughts and the major deals he had pending. One in particular had become too complicated.

"Ugh."

He said he was starting to develop a headache. He swung his body around and planted his feet on the floor. With his back to Ashley he lowered his head into his hands. Ashley stared at him; there is definitely something wrong.

"Babe, what's wrong? Did I do something to upset you?"

"No, I just have a headache. I'll be fine as soon as I take something for it." He said softly. He stood up, grabbed his silk robe off the hook and walked to the living room. He decided against the medicine and got a drink instead. He sat in the dark nursing his drink and headache when Ashley entered the room naked.

"Is there anything I can do to help you?"

"No, go back to bed. I'll be there in a few minutes."

"Okay but don't take too long. The bed is cold without you." She said trying to sound seductive but it came out sounding desperate.

Ivan watched her retreating back as he lay on the sofa putting the glass to his head allowing the coolness to soothe his head. He needed to end this with Ashley permanently. Someone always got hurt even when perimeters were set. She knew this was all she was going to get from him but he could tell that she was becoming attached. The best way to deal with this was a clean break. His thoughts immediately went back to Stephanie. He began imaging them together; making love in several different positions and his entire body began to relax as he dozed off.

CHAPTER FOUR

TUESDAY, JUNE 14th

Stephanie's phone rang just as she was getting off the treadmill. She looked over at the clock it was six o'clock in the morning. It had to be Brianna, Tara, or both.

"Hello," she spoke into the receiver.

"Good morning Ms. Young you don't know how to return phone calls? Brianna asked in a huff.

"Yeah, Miss Anti-social. You didn't call me to find out how my evening went with Lawrence on Saturday."

"Good morning Ladies, I assume since you are calling me in a semi-good mood, that I am still employed."

"Why? What happened?" They inquired in unison. Stephanie explained to the duo the events that happened up until she walked out the door.

"Well, you're a good one considering how rude that bastard was, because I would have cursed his ass out. Tara said irritated.

"She's right Steph. If you feel like he is getting out of hand, you can quit and they can find another agency to use. No one should be verbally abused at work."

"No it's fine, I think he got the message. The one major bonus to this job is the eye candy I get to look at every day. Can I just say that my boss is drop dead gorgeous and he has the most amazing green eyes? I didn't know if I wanted to smack him or sleep with him."

"Yeah right Steph, considering you haven't had sex, how would you know how to start?" Tara said jokingly. There was dead silence on the phone.

"I'm sorry Steph, you know I didn't mean anything by that, I was just joking, obviously badly. I'm sorry, sweetie." Tara said.

"It's fine Ty. I'm just wondering if I will ever find that person that I am willing to share my body with." Stephanie said sadly.

"Or you could be like Tara and give it up to a handsome face and a smile." Brianna said and they all laughed.

"Speaking of giving it up, tell Steph how well you and Lawrence got along." Brianna said.

"Real funny, Bri, but let me just say the brother is packin' and he definitely knows what to do with it." Tara said as she continued to tell them every detail about her night that ended in the morning, including how many times and the different positions. She did not mention the visitor she had after Lawrence left. She still felt a wave of nausea when she thought about how close she came to actually considering a relationship with Dr. Antonio Russo. She shook off the feeling as Brianna's voice interrupted her thoughts.

"Well, that's more than I needed to hear before I've had breakfast."

"Now I'm really ready for a shower, I will talk to you heffas later. Bye." Stephanie said before hanging up the phone.

Stephanie arrived at work early and began to review her assignments as well as comments left by Mr. Quinn from the previous work completed.

"So, I guess this means I'm not fired?" Stephanie said to herself. Betty walked into the office and smiled.

"So I see you made it through the first day, that's more than I can say for some of the previous assistants. Mr. Quinn will be away on business for a couple of days but said you should have enough work to keep you busy for the rest of the week. We are expecting him back on Friday, but there is no guarantee. If you have any questions about the assignments, Mr. Quinn said to speak with his brother Adam. I can introduce you if you'd like? Just between you and me, Adam is much nicer than his brother. He's really handsome and available." Betty said with a smirk.

"Thank you Betty, I'm okay and I have actually met Adam, so the introduction won't be necessary."

"Really," Betty said with a smile as she sat down.

"So did you meet him here or outside of the office?" Betty moved closer to Stephanie as if she were about to be let in on a secret or at least some juicy gossip. Stephanie never liked to gossip or get involved with office politics, so she immediately shut down the conversation.

"I was introduced to him by my employer. So, are those all the assignments on my desk or did Mr. Quinn leave additional ones with you." Stephanie said as she turned from Betty and walked towards her desk. She was not about to tell her that her employer was her best friend and that she met Adam at a nightclub. That would just fan the flames of office gossip. Betty took the hint.

"Yes, but I will have to check my pile to see if he left any additional assignments." She walked away visibly disappointed that she did not get more information.

'Oh, Ms. Betty, I guess you are one of the office gossips and I will have to watch you.'

The next couple of days went by uneventful. Stephanie was extremely busy but enjoyed the work. She was actually getting a feel for what was required in this job and had a pretty good handle on managing the workload. It was Thursday afternoon and Stephanie was finishing up the final touches on her reports. After finishing the final assignment Stephanie sat back, pleased that she had finished everything in record time.

'I guess I will get a chance to explore the other aspects of the company.' Just as she was about to eat the sandwich she packed for lunch, Betty came into the office with a look of panic.

"What's wrong Betty, are you okay?" "No, Ms. Young I..."

"Please, call me Stephanie"

"Uhhh, Stephanie please don't get angry, but I just found two other assignments that Mr. Quinn put on my desk for you to complete and they were under the wrong pile of work."

'Oh just great' Stephanie thought. "Let me see it hopefully I can finish it this afternoon."

Betty gave her the files nervously. "I will stay late to help with whatever I can, I am so sorry, Mr. Quinn is going to be very upset with me."

Stephanie reviewed the files. *'Shit, Shit, Shit, this will take me until midnight to complete.'*

"Ok, Betty let's not panic. If you help me prioritize these assignments we may be able to get it done by tomorrow afternoon."

"But these are the assignments that were to be completed first, Mr. Quinn wants them e-mailed to him by 8:00 am on Friday. I am so sorry I can't believe I missed those folders."

"It's okay, we just need to focus and get to work, but we will have to work late." Stephanie immediately focused on the task at hand and started working, when she looked up again it was nine o'clock and Betty looked exhausted. "Betty, why don't you head home? I can finish the rest and you can come in early to make sure it's e-mailed to Mr. Quinn before eight o'clock."

"No, no I'm fine I want to be here in case you need me to do anything else."

"What you can do for me is put on a pot of coffee and go home to your family, I will be fine."

"Are you sure, this is entirely my fault and I can't believe you are staying to finish this. I will tell Mr. Quinn in the morning that I forgot to give them to you."

"No you won't, they will be ready in the morning to be e-mailed. Now stop worrying and get home because you do have to be here in the morning early."

Betty hugged Stephanie. Never before had anyone at that company been willing to put their neck out there for her and Betty would never forget it.

"I will get the coffee started before I leave and you have my cell number. Call me if you need anything." Betty hesitated before leaving the room. "Thanks again for saving my butt."

Stephanie gave her a faint smile and got back to work.

A few minutes later Stephanie got a cup of coffee and went back to work and exactly an hour later Adam walked by the office and saw the light on, he was surprised to see Stephanie still working.

"You know office hours are from nine to five don't you? Don't tell me my brother has you working this late on your first week."

"No, I just wanted to make sure I completed these reports before I left."

"Well, it's almost ten o'clock do you want me to wait and give you a ride home?"

"I'm fine, I have my car and the security guard has been checking on me. I will only be another hour and then I will be heading out."

"Okay, but know that we are not expecting you to work these types of long hours."

"I know, but I really didn't have any plans so I decided to work late." She did not want to explain to one of her bosses how these assignments were over looked. Adam started to walk away, but suddenly turned around.
"Hey Stephanie, how is Brianna? I was thinking about giving her a call to see if she wanted to go out for drinks."

"She's great, you should give her a call."

"I'll do that and don't stay too much longer." "I won't, good night."

Stephanie looked at her watch and it was eleven thirty. She headed down the hall to the restroom. *I need to review the report one more time and then I can head home, finally.*

When she returned from the restroom she heard someone in Mr. Quinn's office.

'What in the world is going on?' She reached for the phone to alert security. It was then that she recognized the voice.

It was Ivan Quinn. She walked over to her desk, but she could still hear his phone conversation. He was obviously talking to a woman and he was not happy.

"Look Ashley, we've been through this, we agreed no strings. What are you talking about; you benefited greatly from this arrangement so please spare me the victim act. Look, I'm extremely busy and this conversation is over."

He hung up the phone. Stephanie felt like she was eavesdropping although the conversation could be heard clearly throughout the office. She sat at her desk and gathered the files she was working on. She wanted to finish her final review and put them on Betty's desk on her way out. She just needed Mr. Quinn to stay in his office so she could leave before he realized that she was still there. Stephanie did her final corrections and headed towards the door when she heard him.

"What are you still doing here, you aren't expected to stay late." Ivan was surprised that she was still working. He was just thinking about her, *'no wonder the smell of her perfume was still in the air.'* She spun around slightly startled.

"Good Evening Mr. Quinn, I was finishing up a few assignments but I am heading out now."

"Let me see what you were working on"

'Oh, great!' She knew this was not going to be good. She moaned as she handed Ivan the folders, which contained the reports. He quickly glanced at the reports and frowned.

"Why are you just completing these assignments? I left explicit instructions to complete these assignments first. Why are you just getting to these now?" Before she could answer he continued.

"I am really disappointed, if you are having trouble keeping up with the workload then maybe this is not the right job for you." He let out an exasperated breath. "Tell me Ms. Young, are you finding this job too difficult to keep up?" He said with a condescending tone. "I don't have the time or the patience to follow behind my assistants and make sure they are meeting their deadlines. Do I make myself clear Ms. Young?"

She looked up at him with those amazing eyes, the same eyes that haunt him in his sleep. The same eyes he wanted to look into to as he was fucking her, God, he really wanted to fuck her.

"Yes, Mr. Quinn, loud and clear."

'Okay Steph, you had to take this one for the team. Just walk away and keep your mouth shut.' She coached herself.

"It won't happen again. Good night, Mr. Quinn." She turned and heading out the door. She was fuming. 'Every time I run into him it's confrontational. I have truly started off on the wrong foot with him and I need to turn this around.'

Ivan felt bad about the way he spoke to her and he definitely was not ready for her to leave. He wanted to spend more time with her. Before she could get out the office he spoke again, "It is really late, do you need a ride home Ms. Young?"

"No I'm fine, the security guard is going to walk me to my car, thank you for asking." With that said she headed to the security station where Ralph the security guard was waiting.

Ivan went back into his office, poured himself a drink and sat down in his chair. *'I don't know if I can continue to work with her. Why can't I get her out of my mind?'*

Ivan thought he could come into the office late to get some work done without any distractions but there she was and why was she still working. He turned in his chair to look at the city's skyline.

'God she's beautiful.' The thought of her caused his manhood to twitch. *'What the hell is wrong with me?'* He drained the remainder of his drink and began to review the file Stephanie had given him.

"Well, Ms. Young, it appears that you do have a knack for this job." He said aloud.
Her reports were thorough, concise and complete. He had to admit that he could not have done a better job himself. He may have actually found someone whose work impressed him more than Bridget.

When Stephanie walked in her door she went straight to the kitchen. She poured herself a glass of wine, decided to forget dinner, and took a long hot shower.

CHAPTER FIVE

FRIDAY JUNE 17th

Betty walked into the office at seven thirty in the morning ready to email the reports to Mr. Quinn. She searched her desk for the reports when she heard noise coming from Mr. Quinn's office. She entered the office to find Mr. Quinn at his desk.

"Good morning, Mr. Quinn, did you get the reports from Ms. Young?"

"Yes, I did. Thank you."

Betty started to walk out of the office, but then turned around.

"Mr. Quinn, I need to tell you something."

"What is it?" He said sounding irritated, he was not in the mood for office gossip.

"Well, the assignments you left on my desk for Ms. Young..."

"I have them." He replied as he looked up. "Is that all?

"No. I wanted you to know that I did not see the Reynolds's files until yesterday. The folder was under a different pile of work. I gave them to Ms. Young yesterday afternoon, I'm sorry, sir. I thought that I had gone through the pile but I missed those assignments. Betty continued as she stumbled over her words. "I don't want you to be upset with Ms. Young..." He interrupted.

"Well, the reports were handed in on time, so don't worry about it, but going forward we cannot have those kinds of slip-ups. You know the type of work we do here. Everything is time sensitive and one missed deadline could cost this company millions and could cost someone their job. Are we clear?"

"Yes sir." Betty responded.

"Is there anything else, Mrs. Connors?" Betty shook her head and started to walk out of the office. She knew he was angry because he only called her by last name when he was truly upset with her.

"Mrs. Connors, please tell Ms. Young I would like to see her when she gets in."

"Yes sir." She exited the office closing the door behind her.

'So, Ms. Young, you were just given the assignment yesterday afternoon.' Ivan was truly impressed that she was able to turn out such quality work in a short period of time. He could tell by their first conversation that she was feisty and did not have a problem speaking her mind. So why didn't she take the opportunity to correct him when he chastised her about taking this job seriously and questioning her competence? He still couldn't get over the work she produced. Maybe they could work together after all, if he could just keep his hard-on in check for the sake of the company.

Stephanie walked into the office and was immediately greeted by Betty.

"I want to thank you again for yesterday. You did not have to do what you did and I won't forget it. If you need anything just ask."

"Stop Betty, its fine. We got the work done and no one's the wiser."

"Except for Mr. Quinn," Betty blurted out.

"What, how did he find out? Was there a problem with the report?" Stephanie said nervously.

"He knows because I told him. I could not let you take the blame for my mistake."

"That was not necessary Betty, I had it handled."

"Well, he is in his office and he would like to speak with you. Good luck."

Stephanie put here belongs away and knocked on Mr. Quinn's door. "Come!"
She walked into the office and took a seat in front of his desk. His head was down reviewing documents. She spoke first.

"Betty said you wanted to see me." He looked up.

"Yes, it seems I owe you an apology. I had an interesting conversation with Betty, when I spoke with you last night you should have told me that you had just received the assignment. I would not have expected you to complete it in such a short time frame." He waited for a response but there was none so he continued, "With that being said, I was very impressed with your work. There were a few changes but overall job well done.

Stephanie looked into his eyes and she could see the sincerity. She smiled, pleased with herself. "Thank you Mr. Quinn, but..."

"Please call me Ivan."
"Okay Ivan, I do have a few questions regarding your comments on the other reports and I would like to discuss them with you."

Ivan sat back in his chair trying to control the erection he was getting from just listening to her voice.

"No time like the present. Get the reports and we can review them now."

For the next hour they discussed the reports, new assignments and his expectations of his assistants. When the meeting ended, Ivan said,

"It appears I owe you dinner, as both an apology and a thank you for going above and beyond what is expected of you."

"That's not necessary, you don't have to do that."

"I know I don't have to, but I want to and we can make it a working dinner if that will make you comfortable. I can pick you up at seven o'clock."

He stood up indicating that the meeting was over. She walked to the door and spun around before exiting, catching Ivan staring at her ass. He immediately looked up to meet her eyes.

"You don't even know where I live."

"Of course I do. I will pick you up at seven sharp."

He picked up his phone and started dialing. Stephanie looked back then closed the door behind her as she walked towards her desk. *I believe I was just dismissed again.*'

The rest of the day flew by. Ivan came out of his office about two o'clock and told Stephanie to take the rest of the day off because she worked late yesterday.

"Don't forget, seven o'clock sharp." Stephanie gave him a faint smile as she gathered her belongings.

"What's happening at seven o'clock sharp?" Betty whispered. Stephanie started to answer the question but decided against it.

"Wait, what's at seven o'clock sharp?"

"It's nothing Betty. Have a great weekend." She smiled and waved to Betty as she headed out the door.

Stephanie called Brianna on the way home.

"Hey Bri."

"Hey yourself, why are you calling me from your cell phone in the middle of the day? You didn't get fired did you?" She said jokingly. She knew Stephanie was doing a great job because she had just received a report on how wonderful she was working out.

"No, I was given the rest of the afternoon off because I'm doing such a great job and I was also invited to dinner by my boss."

"You are kidding me Steph. You are going on a date with your boss?" Brianna said excitedly.

"Wow, wait a minute no one said it was a date. It's a working dinner, that's all."

"Okay, whatever. You are going out to dinner on a Friday night. Call it what you want. I call it a date."

"Don't start Bri. You know he can barely tolerate me, let alone consider asking me out. It is all about work." Although a small part of her wished it was a date because she considered her boss one of the sexiest men she had ever seen, but she knew she was definitely not his type.

"Hey Bri. What time are you leaving work, I need to talk to you and I would kind of like to do it before dinner with Mr. Quinn."

"Not a problem. Should I call Tara?"

"That would be good, you both can pull me off the ledge." They both laughed.

"See you in a few," Brianna said before disconnecting.

This dinner was bothering her, she was definitely attracted to her arrogant boss and that was a definite NO NO.

Why the hell was he complicating his life even more by taking Stephanie to dinner? He knew when he asked her that it would not be a working dinner, but he needed to see and talk to her outside of the workplace. He didn't understand the strong attraction he had to her. It was definitely a foreign feeling for him and he needed to figure out how to stop it before it became a serious problem.

Ashley was still fuming the next day after her conversation with Ivan. *'If you think that you are getting rid of me that easily Ivan, you need to think again. I know you love me and you don't want to admit it. I won't let you get rid of me because I love you too.'*
She dialed her cell phone and waited.

"Hey, are you still in your office? Good! I need to talk to you. I am heading over now. I'll see you in a few minutes."

The doorbell rang and Stephanie let Brianna and Tara in.

"So what's this I hear about you getting your swirl on with your boss?" Tara said while smiling.

"You can be so crude at times. It's just a business dinner," Stephanie said. "You guys want something to drink?" They said "Wine." in unison. It was five o'clock and she still had time before getting ready for dinner.

"So, what's up Steph, why did you need us to come over?"

"Well, I need some advice. I've told you how handsome Ivan Quinn is, but what I did not tell you is that I really feel a strong connection to him. I mean I can't explain it, but when I'm near him my heart rate speeds up and my palms get sweaty. I don't know if I trust myself around him. I'm not saying I will turn into Tara and open my legs if he smiles at me," she said as she eyed Tara with a smirk before continuing.
"But this is scaring me because he is my boss."

"Real funny, Steph. I am not that easy but I will not deny myself the affections of a handsome man if I am attracted to him." Tara clarified.

"I'm joking Ty. You know I love you, but seriously, I need......" Just then Stephanie noticed that the side of Tara's face was swollen. "Ty what the hell happened to your face." Brianna moved closer to Tara to inspect the bruise.

"What is that?" Brianna said concerned. Tara tried to use makeup to hide it but it was still a little visible. "It's nothing, I was making a cup of tea and left the cabinet door open and walked right into it. It looks worse than it feels."

She was hoping her friends wouldn't question her story because she was close to telling them everything but was too embarrassed and decided against it.

"This isn't about me, it's about your date with your hot boss."

"It's not a date and I do need some advice on handling this situation."

"Wow, I have never heard you talk about any of your ex-boyfriends like this." Brianna said and gave Stephanie a serious look. She continued. "Here's what I think Steph, you are an extremely beautiful, intelligent woman who deserves to be happy. You are always putting everyone's needs ahead of your own. I say if the attraction is there, go for it and let the chips fall where they may." Brianna looked at Tara for confirmation and Tara nodded.

"Okay, Bri I can't believe that we are actually on the same page. You know I am the first to say do what makes you feel good. Life's too short but I do say guard your heart Steph." She said with emphases on her statement. "You tend to open your heart freely and have had it broken in the process. I love you and I just want you to find happiness. Speaking of love and happiness, I have a date tonight with the incredibly handsome and well-endowed Mr. Pierce and with any luck, he will be putting that endowment to work tonight" Tara said as she licked her lips.

"TMI Ty." Brianna said.

"You are such a hoe." Laughed Stephanie. "But seriously thanks guys." Stephanie gave them a group hug. "I guess I better get ready for dinner. I will call you ladies later."

They let themselves out as Stephanie prepared for her working dinner. She decided to wear a wrap-around sleeveless black dress. She gave herself one more look in the mirror before going to the living room. The doorbell rang, Stephanie looked at her watch, *'seven o'clock exactly.'*

Ivan had been sitting in his car for the last fifteen minutes. He could not wait to be alone with Stephanie outside of work; he wanted to give her his undivided attention. To hear her voice, to touch her, to kiss her, to fuck her. *'What the hell is wrong with me? I run a goddamn billion dollar corporation and I can't get my fucking emotions under control with this a woman.'*

He got out of the car and walked into Stephanie's building. She opened the door and inwardly sighed, *'he looks so damn good; this is going to be harder than I expected.'*

"Hello." She said as she turned sideways to let him in.

"Hello yourself. You look absolutely beautiful." That was an understatement. When she opened the door he was blown away by her beauty and the scent she wore was sending his heart rate into overdrive. He had been around beautiful women all his life but there was something special about Stephanie. Looking into her vulnerable and beautiful eyes, he felt an overwhelming need to hold her and protect her from the world.

"Are you ready to go?"

"Yes. Just let me get the lights and lock up."

His 2013 Mercedes-Benz SL65 was parked in front of the building. "Nice car."

"Thank you. It's sort of a hobby."

"Men and their toys." She said just above a whisper.

Ivan smiled and she realized he heard her comment. The ride to the restaurant was quiet. Ivan had classical music playing.

"That's beautiful. Who is it?"

"Her name is Mina. She is an Italian singer from my mom's era. I grew up listening to her. This song is called Non Illuderti, loosely translated it means don't delude yourself about love."

"Oh." Was all Stephanie could say, until Ivan spoke again.

"So, how do you like working for Quinn Corporation considering the few, uhhh, missteps we've had?"

"Missteps? Is that we are calling them?" She smiled. "To answer your questions, the work is demanding but I am enjoying the challenges."

"Like completing a report that should have taken two days in five hours. Very impressive, Ms. Young"

"Well, thank you." She said doing a mock bow in her seat. There was silence again and the music continued to permeate throughout the car. A short time later they pulled in front of Napoli, one of the most exclusive restaurants in Philadelphia. He turned to her before getting out.

"I hope you like Italian."
She smiled at him as the valet opened her door. The smile on her face took his breath away. The restaurant was extremely crowded. The hostess walked up to them as soon as they entered.

"Good evening Mr. Quinn. Would you like your usual table?"

"Yes, that will be fine Maria, thank you."

"Right this way."

She said looking at Stephanie with a faint smile that did not reach her eyes. The restaurant was understated in its design, yet sleek and comfortable. Napoli was designed with a multi-tiered terrace, hand-crafted serpentine bar in the lounge and a cozy lounge setting in front of a roaring fire that added to the romantic atmosphere. From the moment they stepped over the stone threshold. Stephanie could tell a restaurant in Italy must have inspired Napoli.

"I can start you off with drinks. Would you like your usual, Mr. Quinn?"

"Yes." He said as he stared at Stephanie. "And for you Madame."

74

"Oh, I'm not really sure. What do you suggest, Ivan?" "Bring us a bottle of Barolo Pajana and Ms. Young will need a menu."

"Very good sir." And with that she was gone.

"This is a beautiful restaurant and I assume you come here quite often."

"One of my college buddies who is also my best friend owns this place. And yes, I do come here often."

"Well, thank you for bringing me here."

"My pleasure."
"So do you really think we are going to get any work done here? The lights are so dim and the setting is sort of romantic. Under different circumstances this could be considered a date." She said jokingly.

"Do you want it to be?" Ivan said in a serious tone not taking his eyes off of her. Stephanie started to squirm in her seat, suddenly feeling uncomfortable.

"Is that a joke, because I doubt I am your type?"

"Oh, really and what's my type?" He asked staring intently into her eyes. It was hard for her to concentrate with his beautiful green eyes staring as if he could look straight into her soul.

"Oh, I don't know, maybe a beautiful blonde haired, blue eyed model type. Like the one you are pictured beside of in those magazines featuring you as one of Philadelphia's most eligible bachelors." She said sarcastically. Ivan sat back in his chair still not turning away from Stephanie. After a few uncomfortable moments of silence Ivan leaned forward.

"While Ashley is very beautiful, I don't have a specific type and while we are on the subject, we are friends nothing more, nothing less. What about you? Do you have a certain type?"

"My type, uh yeah, that would be losers who leave broken hearts in their path." She said while raising her wine glass to him. "but I'm trying to change my streak." Stephanie thought about her most recent breakup with Mark, a friend from college she reconnected with and started dating. They dated for six months when Stephanie decided to give him her virginity because he already had her heart. She recalled the painful moment, which sent a chill through her.
"You want to talk about it?" Ivan asked clearly seeing the pain in her eyes.

"No, he's not worth my breath."

Their dinner arrived and the conversation lightened as they talked about likes and dislikes families and careers. Once they finished dinner the waitress asked if they would like dessert. Stephanie declined stating she couldn't eat another thing. Just then a very handsome man walked over to the table and sat down.

"Stephanie, this is my friend and the owner of this establishment, Marco Napoli. Marco, this is Stephanie Young."

"It is very nice to meet you Stephanie Young. Such a beautiful lady Ivan. She must be special because I don't ever remember you bringing a date here before." Stephanie could not hide her look of surprise. She wanted to say that it was supposed to be a working dinner not a date, but instead she said. "It's nothing like that, I am Ivan's assistant." Marco looked over at Ivan with a smirk.

"I think it's a little more than that considering the way my dear friend can't take his eyes off of you." Ivan gave Marco a quick glare to indicate that was enough.

"So how long have you been Ivan's assistant, Stephanie?" Marco said, amused at Ivan's reaction. She explained that this was her first week. She also discussed her duties and working relationship with Ivan. The conversation continued between them until Marco excused himself to speak with other patrons.

"Ivan, don't forget about the barbeque on the fourth of July. Maybe you would like to join us Stephanie."

"Thank you, but my two best friends and I were going to throw some burgers on the grill."

"Bring them along. The more the merrier."

"Maybe we will. Thanks for the invitation." She said while looking at Ivan for his approval. Ivan smiled.

"Ivan, you will make sure she gets the address?" Marco said without waiting for a response. "It was very nice to meet you Stephanie, and please don't be a stranger." He said and walked away.
"Would you like another glass of wine?"

"I better not. Two is usually my limit."

"Okay then. I better get you home."

They left the restaurant and drove home, they engaged in small talk as soft music played in the background. When they pulled up in front of her building she turned toward him and thanked him for a wonderful evening. He got out and opened the car door for her and walked with her to her building. They reached the entrance of the building and she turned to him to say goodnight again.

"I'm walking you to your door."

"That's not necessary."

"I insist. I want to make sure you get in your door safely."

They rode the elevator in silence, when they reached her door he took the key from her hand and opened the door.

"Good night Ivan. Thank you again."

He cupped her face with his hands and kissed her softly on her lips. "Good night Stephanie. I will see you on Monday."

Stephanie closed the door leaned against it for support and softly felt her lips as her heart slammed in her chest.

'He is a dangerous man.' She thought and she was going to have to guard her heart closely working with him.

CHAPTER SIX

Ivan walked into his condo poured himself a drink and reflected on his dinner with Stephanie. *'What is it about her that is driving me crazy?'* he walked into his bedroom. "I have to get her out of my head." he said softly.

"Get who out of your head?" Ashley said as she sat up in the bed wearing a white lace bra and matching thong. Slightly startled, then angered, Ivan looked at her.

"What are you doing here and how did you get in?"

"Don't you remember? You have me on the list and the doorman let me in. I thought you would be happy to see me. I haven't seen you in over a week and I thought you might be lonely."

She walked over to him and seductively took a sip of his drink. She put her index finger in the drink and placed her finger in his mouth. He instinctively closed his lips around it sucking the liquid off her finger. He loosened his tie as she unbuttoned his shirt pulled it down his muscular arms and let if fall to the floor. She started kissing him on his chest and then his stomach as she continued downward. He moaned inwardly. She dropped to her knees, unbuckled his belt and unzipped his pants allowing them to pool at his feet. He grabbed her hands before she could release his
manhood from his boxers and pulled her to her feet. He then pulled up his pants,

"We need to talk, have a seat."

Disappointed she sat on the bed with her legs folded under her and listened to him intently as he explained that their arrangement had run its course and they would not be seeing each other again.

As Danny drove her home, Ashley was livid. *'If he thinks I'm just going to walk away, he needs to think again.'* Her plan had to work because she was going to keep him in her life.

Over the next few weeks it was extremely busy and Stephanie loved the distraction. Ivan never mentioned the kiss. They worked together closely but it was strictly a working relationship. There were two major acquisitions the company needed to complete and that meant everyone was burning the midnight oil. The fourth of July was fast approaching and Stephanie and her friends decided to attend Marco's barbeque. Ivan offered to take Stephanie, but she decided to ride with her girlfriends.

MONDAY, JULY 4th

Marco lived in Whitemarsh, a suburb of Philadelphia. The ladies arrived around three o'clock in the afternoon. When they entered the house the party was already in full swing. Stephanie looked around for a familiar face when Marco approached and welcomed her and her friends to his home. He pointed out where the food and drinks were as he walked them to the back of the house, introducing them to other guests. The trio made their way to the bar. They were instantly aware that they were the center of attention. As they walked towards the bar, men eyed them with lustful looks and the women looked at them with envy. The three ladies were brown beauties and they stood out. Tara smiled and whispered to her friends that the song 'Men All Pause' by Klymaxx was playing in her head. They all laughed.

"You would say that Ty." Stephanie said.

When they reached the bar, Marco told them to help themselves to whatever they wanted and to enjoy themselves. Marco turned to Stephanie and said.

"Ivan is somewhere in the house and I will let him know that you arrived." Stephanie just smiled. The ladies got drinks and stood at the bar momentarily until they spotted a free table. As they were approaching the table, Adam and Lawrence walked up behind them.

"The word traveled through the party that three beautiful women have arrived and we had to see what the buzz was about. All I have to say is: Damn, you ladies look beautiful." Lawrence joked. Tara punched him in his arm. "Thanks, I think."

"We are just trying to rescue you ladies because these men look like they are on the prowl and the women look like they are going to pounce." Adam said.

They all laughed as Isabella Napoli, Marco's wife approached. She was a brunette with long flowing hair, a voluptuous figure and model-like features. She introduced herself and welcomed them to her home; she then focused her attention on Stephanie.

"So, I understand that you work for our Ivan. How is that working out?"

As they spoke, Lawrence wrapped his hand around Tara's waist and whispered something in her ear and then they excused themselves. Adam asked Brianna if she was interested in a game of pool and she accepted.

"Now that we are alone, allow me to give you a tour of our home. That should give us a chance to talk." Isabella said with a genuine smile. She hooked her arm into Stephanie's and led her towards the house. Stephanie loved her beautiful Italian accent. She could tell that Isabella was a genuine person and she liked her immediately.

"So, I hear that you and Ivan are dating?" Stephanie looked away not wanting to give her eye contact or she would know how much she really cared for Ivan.

"No, we are colleagues." Stephanie said.

"Me think thou protest too much." She said with a smile. "From what Marco said, he could not keep his eyes off of you at the restaurant and we have never seen Ivan with an actual date other than the usual gold diggers and he has never brought them to the restaurant. I just wanted to meet the woman who has apparently captured Ivan's attention and heart, I can see why. You are an extremely beautiful woman and you definitely have a warm personality." Stephanie smiled shyly and thanked her for the compliment but denied Ivan had feelings for her. "Please dear, the fact that you are here is proof that he has feelings for you."

"I don't understand. Your husband invited me not Ivan."

"But you see dear, the mere fact that you were even at our restaurant means that Ivan cares about you. Trust me, it's a big deal."

"I don't understand."

"Do you like wine?" Isabella inquired.

"Yes." Stephanie said.

"Come, let's have a drink and we can talk in private."

Stephanie and Isabella talked for about 30 minutes before Ivan walked in with Marco.

"You better get your lady before my wife tells all your secrets and starts planning a Christmas wedding." He whispered while laughing. Ivan quickly moved to Stephanie's side.

"Hey." Stephanie turned to see Ivan standing right behind her. She could feel the heat rising in her body. It was crazy how he affected her just by standing close.

"Hey yourself." Stephanie responded.

"May I borrow her Bella? I'm sure you have given her more information that she can handle in a day." Ivan said.

"On the contrary, we were just getting to know each other."
She smiled warmly at Stephanie.

"Well, I would like to speak with her if you don't mind."

"Not at all Ivan. Stephanie I hope we get to continue our
conversation. It was lovely meeting you." She leaned into
Ivan and said. "She's a keeper, don't screw it up." She
kissed his cheek said ciao to both of them and then walked
away.

"Have you eaten?"

"No. I was about to look for Bri and Ty."

"I saw them on the patio with Adam and Lawrence and
they appear to have started without you."

"Well, I guess it's just you and me then." Stephanie said
with a smile. Ivan placed his hand on her lower back as he
led her to the patio. She felt warm all over from his touch.
They got something to eat and found a private table.

"So, how much dirt did Bella dish about me?" Ivan said.
"Actually she had nothing but good things to say about
you." Ivan raised an eyebrow.

"Okay if you say so. How's your food?" He asked while
looking into her eyes.

"It's very good." She said then paused, "Why are looking at
me like that?"

"Like what?" Ivan said not breaking eye contact. Stephanie looked down at her plate, then back into his eyes.

"Like you are looking right through me."

Ivan smiled but didn't answer. As they finished their meal, Brianna, Tara, Adam and Lawrence joined them. "So, are you ladies going to stay for the fireworks, Marco puts on a nice display?" Adam asked.

"Yeah, I guess we can stay for the fireworks but then we have to go. I have work tomorrow and my boss is a hard ass about lateness." Stephanie said smiled shyly and glanced at Ivan and he actually laughed out loud. After the fireworks, Stephanie, Brianna and Tara said their goodbyes and Stephanie promised to stay in touch with Isabella.

WEDNESDAY, JULY 6th

A month into her position, Stephanie along with everyone, was working feverously to complete the final process of the acquisitions. She sat in the conference room with Ivan, Betty, Adam, and Lawrence as they made the final edits to the reports and reviewed the contracts. Finally, they were at a good point to break for the night. Betty reminded everyone about the upcoming formal that the entire office attends every year.

"Will you be attending Stephanie? Mr. Quinn always sends a generous contribution and they send more tickets then we have employees."

"I didn't know I would be invited. I'm not a permanent employee."

"Of course you are invited and you can bring a guest."

Adam said not seeing the glaring look Ivan gave him when he said bring a guest.

"Ok, I will think about it."

Betty was the first to leave followed by Adam and Lawrence who were heading out for drinks to celebrate the completion of the project. Ivan and Stephanie declined the invitation.

Stephanie cleared the paper work in the conference room and headed to Ivan's office to give him the final portion she just completed. She knocked on the door. "Come." Ivan said as he always did when she knocked. She walked into the office and he was at his desk reviewing paper work. He looked up and smiled.

"Come in and have a seat. I need you to review some additional reports if you don't mind staying a little later."

"It's fine. I can stay."

"I already took the liberty of ordering Chinese." Ivan said as he motioned her to sit on the sofa instead of the chair. Stephanie made herself comfortable on the sofa while looking over some paper work. Another hour into working, the food was delivered. Stephanie grabbed a container of Kung Pao chicken, removed her shoes and sat back on the sofa with her feet under her, making sure that her skirt was tucked underneath her. Ivan watched as she positioned herself comfortably on the sofa.

'God she is so beautiful.' Just watching her caused his manhood to pulsate. He grabbed a container of food and sat by her on the sofa.

"Stephanie, is this position something you think you might want to do permanently?"

"Well, this job can be intense but I do like the work and I am really learning a lot about the real estate market. So yes, this is something I can see myself doing long term."

"Good." Ivan said. There was silence. Stephanie was the first to speak. "Can I ask you a something not relating to work?"

"I'm listening." He said while staring directly into her eyes.

"Why did you kiss me a few weeks ago?" He continued to stare into her eyes a few more seconds before he answered.

"You have the most amazing lips. They looked so inviting that I could not resist. After doing so I realized that it was inappropriate and I assure you that it will not happen again unless it is initiated by you." He said confidently.

"Oh really and how do you know I would ever initiate such behavior."

"I don't, but I will not make that mistake again. I am not an impulsive person. Everything I do is thought out thoroughly. So that kiss will not happen again unless it is something that we both agree on." Ivan said.

"Okay good enough."

"Why, Is there a boyfriend I will have to worry about?" He said smiling.

"No. No boyfriend."

"Humph. I do remember that not being a topic you wanted to entertain when we went to dinner. Have your past boyfriends been that horrible?"

"Let's just say that I have on innate ability to attract losers of the lowest kind."

"Care to elaborate? You don't have to if it's too personal or painful."

"I'm sure you don't want to hear about my pathetic personal life."

"Actually I do because I know that you are far from pathetic. So, I would like to know what makes you think your personal life is such."

"Where do I start? Well, let's just say I've always been an assertive person, but for some reason I developed a submissive personality when dealing with men in the past. So while I was in college I decided to be more direct in my approach, but some of my male companions said I was too abrasive. I guess that came from years of being stepped on. When I am pushed to my limit, I severed those relationships. I was definitely not a "let's just be friends" type of person. Anyway after college I tried to find that happy median, with the help of my best friends I think I was able to. I thought I found it in my first real adult relationship with a guy named Mark. He was one of those men that every girl on campus wanted to go out with. He was a real ladies' man. Although I knew about him in college, we did not get together until we had both graduated and I had gone back for our homecoming. We started talking and eventually became a couple, I was determined to make that relationship work.

I really thought I found my soul mate, I had this notion when I was young that I would save myself for my husband. I pictured myself falling in love and my husband would be the only man who would have my heart, body, and soul. But life has a way of smacking you in the face and out of those fairytale views of life. Because I was a virgin when Mark and I started dating I told him I needed time before taking the next step with him. I guess this is TMI {Too much information}." She looked over at Ivan and he was staring at her intently, truly taking in everything she was saying.

"No. Please continue."

"Okay, well my friends thought I was crazy for saving myself. My friend Tara always believed that you should take a test drive the car before it." She smiled when she thought of how many test drives Tara had taken since she'd known her. "Anyway, I decided that it was probably silly to stick to a rule that I had as a young girl. I decided to take that next step with Mark. I planned the entire evening. I planned to come home a day early from a

Conference I had to attend for work. I knew Mark would be at his home because I spoke with him the day before and he said he would be hanging at the house all evening. So I ordered food to be delivered from one of our favorite restaurants. I bought this ridiculously expensive lace bra and panty set with garter, thigh-high stockings, and stiletto heels." She looked at Ivan and he had a lustful look in his eyes and she thought to herself maybe I shouldn't be sharing this story with my boss, so she decided to end the story. "Well I guess you can tell it didn't ...." Sensing her uneasiness Ivan encouraged her to continue.

"Please Stephanie I would like to hear the end of the story." She looked him in the eyes and could see that he was genuine. "Okay." She stood and looked out at the city skyline and continued the story without looking at Ivan.

"I went straight home from the airport; I changed into the undergarments I purchased, put on a thin coat and headed over to Mark's place. Early on in our relationship we exchanged keys to each other homes, so I let myself in. I heard soft jazz music playing which was a clear indication that he was home and was probably working in his office on the second floor. I was so nervous; I had butterflies in my stomach. I was actually going to give myself to him and while this was not a big deal for some women, it was for me. I steadied my nerves and walked up the stairs thinking how surprised Mark is going to be that I actually decided to make the first move. As I mounted the stairs I thought I heard something, I dismissed it as probably being the television. I heard noise from his bedroom." She paused a few seconds and Ivan could see that the hurt was still fresh. Stephanie turned from the window and sat back on the sofa putting her feet under her, this time not paying attention to her skirt, which was raised up to her upper thigh. Ivan immediately noticed, but turned away trying to concentrate on Stephanie's story. Stephanie saw something in the way Ivan looked at her. She felt like she could trust him with this private, intimate moment in her life so she continued.

"I was about to open the door when I heard a familiar female voice. It still was not registering in my brain what I was actually hearing. I turned the doorknob and there they were, my boyfriend pounding my ex-friend from work. I stood there in total shock with my coat opened revealing most of me as if I was invited to join them in on a threesome. I immediately felt sick to my stomach and all I could do was yell, "Mark, what are you doing?" They both turned to see me drop to my knees; he looked over at me and asked me what I was doing there. Really what I am doing here? Not 'I'm sorry you caught me fucking your friend from work' or 'I'm sorry for being unfaithful', but what are you doing here. I wanted to scream at both of them, I wanted to fight but all I could do is run to the bathroom and empty the contents of my stomach. Mark ran into the bathroom behind me asking me if I'm okay and I thought what a stupid ass question, of course I'm not okay. I rose to my feet with my coat open and he looked at the outfit and I guess it dawned on him why I was there. He immediately began to apologize telling me that this was the only time and it would never happen again; the only thing I could do was smack him across his face before running down the steps and out of the house. He ran after me, naked, trying to get me to calm me down. I was so angry that if I had stopped, I would have turned around and went back to beat both their asses. As I ran through the door with my coat open, the delivery guy with the food from the restaurant was there. It wasn't until I saw his eyes glued to me that I realized he could see almost every intimate part of me. I looked at the delivery guy, totally unashamed of my appearance. With my hands on my hips, I told the delivery guy to give the food and the bill to the lying cheating son of a bitch standing behind me."

She stood again and walked over to the window to see the Philly night skyline. She was trying to hold back her tears. "That was the last time I opened my heart to someone fully. It's just not worth the hurt and pain." Ivan's heart broke for her and he hated seeing her in pain. He also felt the anger building for the man who would hurt her that way.

"I later found out that Mark had several women he was sleeping with, but what I didn't understand was why he gave me a key to his place. Who does that? I mean if you are screwing anything in a skirt why give me a key and risk me finding out?"

Ivan sat silent while she talked he realized that she was not really asking questions for answers but merely venting.

"So that's the whole sordid story. I am currently not with anyone because I have not have found anyone I trust with both my heart and body. A little pathetic, huh?" She said as she turned toward him. He walked over to her standing so close she could feel his body heat. Ivan used his bent index finger to lift her head.

"Not at all. I am sorry that happened to you, you are an extremely intelligent beautiful woman and obviously too good for that ass you dated. I think that eventually you will find the right person." She looked into his green eyes. "Thank you for saying that." She took a step back and turned towards the sofa, she did not trust herself to be so close to Ivan. She definitely wanted to kiss him. "What about you? Any broken hearts to speak of?" She said trying to calm her nerves.

"Not really, I am not big on the whole relationship thing."

"What does that mean, relationship thing?" Before he could speak, the door opened and in walked a tall beautiful woman. Stephanie recognized her from the photos in the magazines with Ivan. She had long blonde hair and deep blue eyes. Ashley gave Stephanie a once over and turned her nose up before returning her attention to Ivan. Ivan tried to contain his anger. "Why are you here, Ashley?" Stephanie saw that as her cue to leave. "Well, if we are done here Mr. Quinn." He interrupted. "Ivan." Stephanie smiled slightly and continued, "Ivan, if you don't need me anymore I'm going to head home."

"No, he won't need you anymore this evening." Ashley glanced down at her watch.
"It's probably past your bedtime." She said snidely. Stephanie rolled her eyes wanting to tell her exactly what she could do with her 'bedtime' but decided against it.

"Stephanie, give me a minute. I will take you home."

"That won't be necessary. I can take a cab."

"Yes, Ivan, let her take a cab." Ashley hissed.

"Stephanie give me a few minutes and I will take you home," he said with such authority that Stephanie nodded in agreement.

"Okay, I will run to the ladies room and meet you back here in a few minutes."
He looked over at Stephanie with a soft expression and said. "Thank you."

Stephanie walked out of the office closing the door behind her. She grabbed her phone to call Bri. The phone rang one time and went to voice mail. 'Her meeting must have run late,' Stephanie thought as she glanced at the time. 'I'll call her later.'

CHAPTER SEVEN

"Ms. Robinson you will have to leave now if you want to make it in time for your four thirty appointment at O'Hara restaurant."

"Huh, how is it you let me schedule a meeting so late in afternoon?"

"Sorry, but it was the only time that fit into your schedule."

"Okay, give me ten minutes and call the client to confirm the appointment; I don't want to go all the way over there only to find out that they canceled."

A few minutes later the appointment was confirmed and she was heading out the door.

He was so close, Brianna could feel the heat from his body and his warm breath tickled her neck, he inhaled deeply.
"Damn Bri, you smell so good," he said before his mouth connected with hers. The kiss was so intense that Brianna could feel the wetness pooling in her panties, she moaned. His tongue moved around in her mouth, she could taste the alcohol. He captured her tongue and sucked on it until her mouth watered. He was so turned on he had a hard time getting the door open to his condo. Once the door was opened he pulled Brianna inside before closing the door with his foot. Brianna cupped his face with her hands and pulled his lips back to hers then wrapped her arms around his neck and her legs around his waist as he backed her into the nearest wall causing pictures on the end table to

fall over. He grabbed her ass as he pulled her into his throbbing erection.

"Oh my god, this is so not professional, I don't do this, EVER," she said as she started breathing heavily. He pulled her blouse over her head and unsnapped her bra allowing her beautiful full breasts to fall. He captured her nipple with his teeth and lightly bit down on it right before running his tongue along to soothe the
sting. She was becoming undone as he continued to grind his erection into her moist center.

"Oh my god I'm coming I'm....." Before she could utter another word, tremors shook her entire body. *'Shit'* she was not out of her panties and she already had
an orgasm.

"I want you so bad, Bri, it hurts. Tell me to stop, tell me to stop now before we get to the bedroom." He said while carrying her to the bedroom.

"I want you, I want you inside me now." Brianna said, barely able to catch her breath. He dropped her on the bed. "You are so beautiful," he said as his eyes grazed over her entire body. He knelt in front of the bed and pulled her body towards him; he hooked his finger on the waistband of her white lace panties and slid them down her legs. He inserted a finger in her pussy; she moaned and closed her eyes grinding herself into his finger. He withdrew his finger and licked her juices off of it.

"You are so wet," he said as he lowered his head, kissing her other set of lips. With his nose touching her clit he inhaled taking in her womanly scent, he loved her smell.

He ran his tongue along the length of her pussy, he felt her shiver. He smiled as he began to suck, lick, and kiss her beautiful pussy. "I could get addicted to this," he whispered. He continued to suck her juices as she fisted his hair trying to pull him even closer as she grinded on his face. He inserted his tongue in her heat as he used his first two fingers to rub her swollen clit in a circular motion. He continued to thoroughly tongue fuck her until she screamed his name out from another orgasm slamming into her. He held her in place as her body stopped trembling; he quickly shed his clothes, sheathed himself with a condom and mounted her, entering her with one swift thrust. She screamed with pleasure as he stayed motionless so that her body could adjust to his size. "You are so wet and so tight." He was losing every shred of control he had. She wrapped her legs around his waist.

"God, you feel so good. Please move now." She said as she thrust her hips forward.

"FUCK." he moaned as he pulled out and thrust back into her, it took a few seconds to get their rhythm, but once they did, the sex was amazing. Brianna felt the pressure building again.

"Oh my god, I going to cum again."

He could feel her muscles tighten around his manhood. He lost it, pounding her until he came a few seconds later. He collapsed on her chest breathing heavily. Brianna could not believe how good it felt. It had been too long since she last got laid and it was long overdue. He was by far the best lover she had ever had, not that she had that many, but he was definitely the best. He rolled over on his back, removed the condom and placed it in the trash. He turned towards Brianna.

"Bri, that felt so good." He said as he caressed her face and tucked a fallen curl behind her ear.

"I am not in the habit of doing one-night stands." She said as her breathing and heart rate calmed down.
"Who says it has to be one night, I want to see you again Brianna." He said as he pulled her into the spooning position. Brianna was so tired that all she could do was nod before she dozed off.

Ivan turned to Ashley. "I'll ask you again. Why are you here?" Ashley spoke with venom in her voice.

"Oh, you just discard me like yesterday's trash. I thought I meant more to you than that." Ivan stared directly into her eyes.

"And what gave you that impression?" Ivan asked.

"What?" Ashley said confused.

"You heard me Ashley, what gave you the impression you meant more to me? I sure as hell didn't." He walked over to Ashley and in an even low tone said. "This will be the last time we have this conversation. We had an arrangement, that's all, which I might add you benefited from handsomely. I get the credit card statements. Did you think I would not notice that you spent over two hundred thousand dollars at Tiffany's or the eighty thousand dollars you spent on shoes and clothing. I knew you were a self-centered, conniving, opportunistic gold digger, but did I complain? No. Because I knew who and what you were the first time I fucked you on your desk."

Ashley gasped at his harshness. "You agreed to this arrangement, we had a deal and now it's over. Now, as we agreed you will keep the condo and the Volvo. But you will be responsible for the maintenance of both. I will arrange to have them both transferred into your name, but I have canceled the credit cards. This is goodbye, Ashley."

He walked back over to his seat but before he could sit down she yelled. "Who is that pretty black bitch out there Ivan, are you fucking her now?"

Ivan turned and moved so fast closing the gap between them that it startled her. He stood in her personal space, barely raising his voice above a whisper. "This is my place of business, don't you ever disrespect me or one of my employees ever again or you will find yourself out in the street and without a car and I will make sure that you never find gainful employment in this city again. Don't. Test. Me. Ash. You. Will. Lose." Ashley stepped back frightened. She had never seen this side of Ivan before.

"Now I will say it one last time. Goodbye Ashley."

With tears in her eyes she mouthed that she was sorry and left the office. Ivan hated hurting Ashley, but she was the type of woman that would not go away with a soft nudge. She needed a firm push to get the message. Stephanie passed Ashley in the hall. She looked over at Stephanie and yelled. "What are you looking at?" As she continued down the hall. Stephanie was too stunned to answer. She walked back into her office and Ivan was standing there with his jacket in hand.

"You ready?" Ivan said as if a beautiful woman did not just leave his office crying hysterically.

"Yeah, let me grab my things." She stared at him as they walked to the car.

"What." He said waiting for the questions.

"Nothing. It's none of my business." She responded. They drove to her house in silence. Just as he was about to park in front of her building she had to ask.

"Okay, so I'm going to ask. Who is she?" Stephanie asked as she turned in her seat presumably getting comfortable for a lengthy response. He turned the car off and shifted in his seat.

"She used to be a friend and now she's not, end of story." He said with little emotion.
"She did not seem happy about not being your friend anymore. There has to be more. You can tell me it's none of my business." Ivan looked into her eyes, silently feeling the need to bare his soul. After a few seconds he shifted forward and spoke.

"Stephanie, all of my adult life I have been driven to succeed, my brother and I started this company ten years ago and I eat, sleep, and breathe our company initially working seven days a week. I was so driven I did not have time for relationships. When our business took off and we were in papers and magazines touted as the up and coming leaders in the business world I started getting unwanted attention from women looking for a husband or benefactor. Since I had no intention of getting married any time soon, if ever, I started seeing only women who were willing to abide by my rules. My main rule was: no relationships, just agreements or arrangements."

"What does that mean? Agreements. And was the blonde woman part of one of these agreements?" She knew that she was being extremely forward, but she needed to know almost like her future depended on it. "Wow. You have a lot of questions." He smiled but continued, "Well, when I see a woman I am attracted to and she is attracted to me I let her know upfront that I am not looking for a relationship just a sexual partner and an occasional companion when I have to attend different events. In exchange, uh, let's just say, I am a very generous man. I give them what they want
and they give me what I want."

Stephanie looked at him in disbelief. "So basically you're talking about prostitution," she said with the sarcasm rolling off her tongue.

"No, Stephanie, it is not prostitution, it is an arrangement between two consenting adults who are not interested in anything more."

"And you think these arrangements or agreements don't have its share of problems, because when emotions are involved and trust me when sex is involved there is always emotions, someone gets hurt even when that is not your intention, like the blonde at your office."

"Well, up until now it has not been an issue. Ashley, uhh..that's the blonde, wants more than I can give her."

"Oh, I see. Well, good night Ivan." She said not wanting to continue the conversation because she could feel herself getting upset and she did not want to argue with him.

"Why are you leaving? I thought we were talking."

She looked at him, he could sense she wanted to say more but she said nothing. He moved in closer and brushed his lips lightly against hers. Her body began to tingle, she moved in closer to return the kiss. Ivan took her face in his hands and kissed her so hard and deeply she started to feel dizzy.

"WOW, all right, we need to stop. Look, Ivan, I want to say something to you and I hope it does not jeopardize my job."

"I thought we were speaking freely and of course your job would not be in jeopardy." Ivan said sincerely.

"Okay, I don't know how to say this other than just coming right out with it. First, I like you; I also like to be upfront with people about what I want and trust me Ivan, I want you. I mean, I am really developing strong feelings for you, but I can't be one of your arrangements. I'm not built that way. So whatever this is that we are doing we should stop because I am looking for a committed relationship, not an agreement or an arrangement."

Ivan looked into her eyes. "I don't know if I can give more than that." Stephanie's body stiffened and he could feel it.

"Well, I guess we both have our answer then, don't we. We shouldn't do this anymore, this...taking me home, kissing me." Her voice started to crack. "I like working with your company and I think that we need to keep our relationship strictly professional because I can't do this. Good night Ivan."

Before he could respond she jumped out of the car and ran into her building not looking back. She opened her door, slammed it and leaned against it for support.
"Great! What were you thinking, you just told your boss you had feelings for him. Stupid. Stupid. Stupid." She said to herself while smacking herself on her forehead with the palm of her hand. She reached for her cell phone. It was late but she needed to talk to Bri.

Ivan sat in his car stunned. "What did she just say, she had feelings for me?" He smiled at that thought then his smile turned solemn. "I can't do this. I don't do relationships." This woman was turning his life upside down. When was that last time he sat in a car having a long conversation and making out like a lovesick puppy? Uh, never. He reached for his cell phone. "Hey. Are you busy? I need to talk to you. I'm on my way over." Ivan closed the phone and pulled off. When Ivan arrived the door was already open and he walked in. Adam stood in his living room with two drinks in his hand. Ivan took the glass that was extended to him and drained it. He walked over to the bar to make another drink.

"So, big bro, you want to tell me what's wrong." Ivan sat on the sofa and looked at his brother who was in a robe.

"Did I interrupt something? Look, I'm sorry, I will leave. We can talk tomorrow."

"No, no. its fine." Adam said and looked towards his bedroom. "What's up?" Adam asked.

"I don't know what's happening to me. She constantly invades my thoughts. I can't stop thinking about her and when I'm near her I have this uncontrollable urge to hold her." Ivan was rambling. Adam looked at his brother. "Who Ashley?"

Ivan glared at him "No Stephanie." Ivan corrected.

"Wait, your assistant Stephanie?" Adam said confused again looking towards the bedroom door before returning his attention to Ivan. Ivan took another sip of his drink.

"Yes, my assistant. There is something definitely wrong with me. When I see her, my heart literally skips a beat; what the hell is going on with me? I don't know what I am going to do. I just ended things with Ashley because she started to become too clingy, but with Stephanie it's different. You know the last time I slept with Ashley I kept seeing Stephanie's face."

Adam looked at him and smiled. *'Cupid has finally bit my brother in the ass'.* "What do you want me to say?" Adam asked.

"I want you to tell me how to get rid of these feelings." Ivan huffed.

"Well, the way I see it, Ivan, you have two choices. You can fire her, because trust me bro these feeling will not go away as long as you work so closely with her."

"So what is my second option?" Ivan asked.

"Your second option is to pursue a relationship and see where it goes."

"Come on Adam, you know I can't do that, my life is too complicated right now with everything that's going on with the company. I don't have the luxury of pursuing a relationship."

"That's bullshit Ivan and you know it. You choose not to pursue relationships because it's easier that way. You hook up with these women and when they start to get close, you dump them on the pretense that it's part of some agreement. You know what I think." Before he could finish they both turned their heads as they heard a cell phone ringing in the bedroom.

"Do you need to get that?" Ivan asked.

"No. It's not my phone." Ivan gave him a knowing look.

"Anyway, like I said I think you are afraid to put yourself out there for fear that you will get hurt."

"See, that's where you are wrong little brother because I'm not afraid of a goddamn thing, least of all a woman." Ivan growled.

"Prove it, if you feel that strongly for Stephanie pursue a relationship with her. A real relationship and not that bullshit you've been involved in the past." Ivan looked at his brother "I don't know, maybe you're right."

Ivan sat his glass down. "I better head out, I have get to the office early. Besides I think your company is awake." Ivan hugged his brother. "Thanks for the advice. I'll see you tomorrow." Ivan got into his car still confused about what he was going to do.

"Hello?" Brianna said in a hushed, groggy tone. It took her a few seconds to realize where she was. "Shit." Brianna said softly realizing where she was.

"What's wrong Bri?" Stephanie said.

"Nothing. Is everything ok? It's really late." Brianna whispered.

"Why are you whispering, where are you? Did I interrupt something? Bri, I am so sorry, call me tomorrow." Stephanie's rapid-fire questions had Brianna's head spinning.

"No....no, it's fine, I have a few minutes. Uh, what's wrong?" Brianna asked trying to contain a yawn. Stephanie described her evening with Ivan and as usual Bri talked her off the preverbal ledge and made her feel better. Adam walked back into the room.

"Steph, I have to go. We will talk tomorrow." She said while eyeing Adam's body as he disrobed and got back in the bed.

"Ok, have fun and do everything I wish I could do." Stephanie jokingly said.

"Will do." Brianna said while disconnecting the call without another word, never taking her eyes off of Adam as he moved between her legs.

Stephanie hung up the cell phone feeling better about her situation and wondered whom Bri was with. She always felt more grounded once she talked to her girl.
'I know what I have to do.' She smiled, as she got ready for bed.

CHAPTER EIGHT

THURSDAY, JULY 7th

Stephanie was dressed and waiting for Ivan, since her car was still at work. She decided to have a conversation about how they intended to handle their attraction to each other. If he was not interested in a relationship, then their relationship would strictly be a professional one: no dinners, no more rides home and definitely no more kissing. God, she loved the way he kissed. She started feeling warm just thinking about him. The doorbell rang, *'here we go'* she thought. She opened the door and to her surprise Danny, Ivan's driver, was standing there.

"Good morning, madam, you ready to go?" He said in a chipper voice.

"Where's, Ivan?" Stephanie asked.

"He asked me to pick you up. He had to be in the office before 7:00 a.m. Are you ready?"

'So, you're trying to avoid me Mr. Quinn? Well, that's fine with me.'

Stephanie was so busy at work that she looked at the clock and realized it was 4:00 p.m. There was no sign of Ivan. She finished up her assignments and headed home.

FRIDAY, JULY 8th

Stephanie arrived at work and her desk was piled with assignments that needed to be done immediately, she delved in to her work. She did notice that Ivan was in his office but she was so busy she did not even think about Ivan and the conversation she needed to have with him. The day flew by and before she looked around again the day was done and according to Betty, Ivan had apparently left for the day. *'Well, I guess we won't have that conversation today, but we will resolve this thing between us Ivan.'* She said to herself as she left the office to meet her friends for dinner.

Stephanie arrived at the restaurant early and decided to get a table and have a drink while she was waiting. She was deep in thought when she heard a deep voice, "Hello stranger." Lawrence said bringing her out of her thoughts.

"Hey Lawrence, long time no see. How's life treating you or better yet, how's Tara treating you?"

"I'm glad you asked. Do you mind if I sit?" He said.

She motioned her hands for him to have a sit. "So, what are you doing here?" Stephanie asked.

"I just finished up with some clients. So, why are you eating alone?"

"I'm actually early, waiting for my girls."

"Speaking of your girl, what's up with her? I thought we were getting along but now she won't return my calls, is everything okay with her?"

"Yes, she's fine but if you hang around for about a half an hour she should be here."

"I wish I could wait but I am heading to another late meeting. Tell your girl I will call her later and if she doesn't take my call I'm going to camp outside her house." He said jokingly. He rose, gave Stephanie a kiss on the cheek and told her to take care of herself.

Ivan walked into the restaurant and immediately noticed Stephanie sitting at the table with Lawrence. *'What the Hell....'* He thought *'What are they doing here together?'* Ivan felt his temperature rise. He was suddenly consumed with jealously. He needed to calm himself down before he approached them or it could turn ugly. He ordered a drink from the bar he took a sip as he walked towards the table. As he was approaching he saw Lawrence kiss Stephanie. *'Are they seeing each other? I'll be damn if I'll allow him to steal my woman. My woman? She is not my woman, at least not yet, but she will be.'* Just as Ivan arrived at the table Lawrence was about to step away when Ivan halted his process. Lawrence looked up. "Hey, Ivan, what's up?"

"That's funny. I was about to ask you the same thing."

He said looking back and forth between the two with a disgusted look on his face.
Lawrence looked at Ivan puzzled. "Look, I'm not sure what's going on, but I have to get to a meeting. Ivan, I will

talk to you later and Stephanie, don't forget what I told you. Later." Stephanie smiled as Lawrence walked away.

"So, the elusive Mr. Quinn is around," she said with sarcasm.

"What the hell was that about?" Ivan said through his teeth obviously seething.

"What was what about?" she said looking into his green eyes that seemed to be getting darker. *'Is he jealous?'* She thought.

"Don't be coy, Stephanie. You know exactly what I'm talking about, you and Lawrence. Are you seeing him now only a day and a half after confessing your feelings for me, or has this been going on all along?" *'He is jealous.'* She sat silently while he continued on his tirade.

"So how long have you been seeing him? Are you trying to play both of us?"
Now it was her turn to get angry.

"Play you? Play you?"

She said a little louder then she intended. She looked around to see if anyone was looking and focused her attention back to Ivan.

"You've got some damn nerve to approach me with this bullshit. You are the one who's been avoiding me for the last couple of days." She said through her teeth, trying not to cause a scene. "Yes, I told you how I felt, but I also told you it's all or nothing. I am not doing any agreement." Ivan stood there, a little stunned by her reaction as she continued. "And now you come over to my table, implying that I am seeing someone else after I told you how I feel about you. You have the nerve to question my character while trying to stake your fucking claim on something that is not yours." Stephanie was so angry that tears threatened to fall but she refused to give him the satisfaction of seeing her cry.

"Do you remember our last conversation? I sure as hell do. I believe it was you who said that you could not do a relationship. So why are you now questioning who I chose to date?"

Ivan remained silent as his piercing green eyes bore into her.

"So, you are dating him." He said in a low irritated tone. She was about to answer when her girlfriends approached the table. Ivan never took his eyes off of Stephanie.
Tara cleared her throat. "Are we interrupting something?"
Stephanie looked up; her friends could tell that something was wrong.

"No, Mr. Quinn was just leaving." Ivan stood.

"It's a pleasure to see you both again. Stephanie, we will finish this conversation later." He said as he walked away from the table without a backwards glance.

"What was that about? It looked pretty intense when we walked up." Brianna said as they both sat down. Stephanie gave them a recap of what just transpired before they arrived. When they started to offer opinions, she shut down the conversation. Stephanie just wanted to eat and enjoy her friends who she had not seen in a while. Changing the subject, she turned to Tara and said, "What did you do to Lawrence? He is completely sprung." They laughed and Tara talked about their situation. They finished dinner, said their goodbyes and Tara promised to call Lawrence.

Tara arrived home and was having second thoughts about calling Lawrence. She really liked him and he needed to know about her past relationship before she could move forward with a serious relationship with him. She knew he wanted more but she didn't know if she could offer more. Her past relationship with Dr. Antonio Russo really affected how she viewed relationships. She was scared. She picked up the phone and dialed Lawrence's number.

"Hi." She said when he answered the phone.

"How are you? He responded.

"Not good, look I need to talk to you about something and I need to do it tonight before I lose my nerve."

He could tell by the nervousness in her voice that it was serious. "What is it?" He said a little taken aback by the tone of the conversation.

"Not over the phone can you come over?"

"I'm on my way."

Fifteen minutes later Lawrence was at Tara's door. He walked in and she led him to the sofa. "I know I have been acting strange lately, but there is a reason why I have been avoiding you." She stood; her nervous energy had gotten the best of her.

"You want a drink, let me get us both a drink." Before he could respond she headed towards the kitchen. *'What the fuck is going on?'* He thought. She came back with two glasses of wine and the wine bottle. He took his glass and the bottle and prompted her to sit down. She sat next to him and drained her glass.

"Damn Ty what is wrong?"

She blew out a breath and sat close to him not giving him eye contact. "Okay, I know that you've been wondering what has been wrong with me and why I keep canceling our dates. I also know that you want more from our relationship, but you need to know why I am so gun shy when it comes to relationships. I need to tell you something that I have not even told my best friends."

"Okay." Lawrence said.

"Several months back I ended a relationship with a man who started to become abusive." Tara could feel Lawrence's body stiffen. She turned to face him she could see he was getting angry. She continued. "My friends did not know we were dating because he was Italian and I did not know how they would react to me dating someone of a different race. Kind of silly huh? Well anyway we went out for about three months when we had our first big argument I can't even remember what the argument was about, but I do remember the bruise he left on my face."

"What's his name Ty?" Lawrence said trying to contain his anger.

"That's not important, I just need you to hear me out so you understand why I have been acting the way I have." Lawrence put his arm around her shoulder as she continued. "Our first night together was actually the first time I slept with someone since my break up. I just want you to know that night was amazing." She smiled at him and she could see his face soften. "Anyway, when you left that morning, I was about to take a shower when the bell rang and I thought you forgot something." Tara began to detail the events that happened as she relived that morning..........

"Did you forget something or just miss... What are you doing here?

"You don't seem excited to see your fiancé? He said.

"You are not my fiancé or did you not get the hint when I threw the ring back at you." I screamed.

"Come on Ty, I know you have missed me as much as I have missed you. I thought I would give you some space and time to reconsider your rash decision. After all, I do love you and I know you love me. One bad decision on my part should not destroy our entire relationship."

"Relationship, relationship, there is no relationship. You did a good job of destroying that four months ago. You need to leave." As I spoke he closed to gap between us and pulled me into him in a gentle warm embrace. The warm comforting feeling I use to get from him was now turned into a sickening feeling in my stomach. I pulled

away from him and kept a safe distance.

"You need to go, I meant it when I said we are done."

He reached for me again and I flinched my arm back. He sighed, "I understand, you need more time."

"I don't need more time I just need you to leave now."

"Okay fair enough but can I at least use the little boys room before I go?" He smiled at me and I nodded. He walked into the powder room as I walked back towards the kitchen. After a few seconds I heard the door to the powder room swing open so hard it hit the wall. He came barreling out storming towards me "Who the hell are you fucking?" Before I could move his fist came crashing down on my face. My head slammed against the floor I felt nausea and dizziness cover me all at once. I tried to crawl away as he knelt down with the condom wrapper in his hand. He grabbed me by the collar of the silk robe I was wearing. "I cannot believe after everything we have been through you would do this shit to me. You are such a fucking whore, you know what happens to whores." He stood me up, my head was swimming everything seemed to be going in slow motion. Before I could get my bearings he pulled me over to the sofa and ripped my robe from my body leaving me completely nude. He slammed my body against the sofa and started to undo the belt on his pants. Tears started to stream down my face.

"So you're going to rape me." I said angrily. "Is that what you want, you are such a pussy." I yelled. "I swear to god if you rape me you better kill me because I will call the police and have them arrest your ass and you better hope they get to

you before my brother does." He froze looking into my eyes. He sat down on the sofa slumped over with his face in his hands.

"God, I am so sorry Ty, I don't know what came over me. He looked at me. I sat up pulling my knees to my chest and wrapping my arms around my legs trying to hide my nakedness. I was determined not to should how truly frightened I really was. "I thought we were going to work through our problems and then I saw the condom wrapper and I went crazy. Please baby forgive me, I promise I will never put my hands on you again. Give me another chance, give us a chance." A tear started to fall down his face. He tried to hug me but I flinched back. "You need to leave now and I never want to see you again." I said barely above a whisper. "If you try to call me or come by again I will press charges and get a restraining order against you. So if you value your precious reputation and career you will leave me alone."

"You don't mean that Ty you know I love you."

I could feel my fear turning to anger. "You are confusing delusional love with real love. Real love does not require you to beat my ass because I don't do something you like. I told you when you hit me the first time we were done. You are truly delusional if you think that there can ever be an "us" again. You killed that when you hit me four months ago. Now please leave." He opened his mouth to say something then decided against it, instead his kissed my forehead walked to the door and left without looking back. I stood up steadied myself, walked to the door and locked it. I walked up the stairs slowly feeling pain reeling throughout my body. I had to hold onto the rail going up the stairs so that I could keep my balance. I walked directly into the bathroom and turned on the shower. I stepped into the shower and let the hot water spray all over my body. I tilted my face upward feeling the stinging pain of blow I took from the man who professed to love me. I remember sliding down the shower wall onto the shower floor lying in a fetal position and sobbed loudly. I cried because of the pain I felt in my body, the pain I felt mentally and the pain I felt in my heart. How could I have loved a man who hurt me physically, mentally, and emotionally? I was so shocked and ashamed the first time he hit me that I did not tell anyone not even my best friends, but I was not going to be a victim and I was definitely not going to stay with a man who hits me. I dragged myself out of the shower and got in my bed where I stayed all weekend ignoring several calls I received from my friends and you.

Lawrence stood no longer able to contain his anger. "What's his fucking name Ty?" He said louder than he wanted to.

"I'm not telling you this story so that you can fight my battles for me I just want you to know that place I am coming from so hopefully we can move past it. "Babe I cannot stand by and knowingly let someone put their hands on you so I'm going to ask you again, what's his name?"

"I'm not going to tell you because I don't want you to end up in jail because of me. I just want to know if you are still willing to give me a chance knowing that you will have to be patient with me?" Lawrence looked into her eyes and wondered how anyone could hurt someone so beautiful.

He grabbed her by her waist and pulled her into a gentle hug.

"I really care for you Ty and yes I can be patient." He kissed her so gently that her heart melted. He lowered himself onto the sofa and pulled her into his lap. He rubbed her hair and back softly. "I want you to know that I will never put my hands on you other than to love you and to make love to you. I would never hurt you." He kissed her forehead as she lay on his chest allowing him to comfort her. She didn't know how long she was in that position before she fell asleep. Lawrence could not sleep he could only think about finding the animal that abused her and give him a taste of his own medicine. Starting tomorrow he would find out who he was and make him pay.

When Stephanie arrived home her cell phone rang. It was Ivan. She answered it.

"Yes?"

"Are you home?"

"Yes."

"I'm on my way up." With that he hung up the phone. The doorbell rang and she opened the door.

"Come in." He walked towards the sofa and sat. "Would you like something to drink?"

"No." He said as he sat silently.

"So, you're here. Talk." She said getting frustrated.

He took a deep breath. "Are you seeing him?"

"What?"

"Answer the damn question, Stephanie. Are you seeing him?"

"You know you've got a lot of nerve. First, you come to my house unannounced. Then you demand answers to questions you have no right to, but for the record, no, I am not seeing Lawrence. He and Tara are dating and he was asking me questions about her when you walked over." Stephanie said with anger in her tone, blinking back tears. Why does she allow him to affect her? Ivan looked at her and he felt like a ton weight had been lifted off of his chest. He sighed deeply and walked over to her using his thumb to wipe away a tear that escaped. His entire left hand encased the right side of her face as he pulled her into a kiss. The kiss was soft but quickly deepened unleashing the passion he felt for her. His tongue delved into her mouth, coaching her tongue into his. They both moaned as Ivan reached under her tank top grabbing her breast, she felt her body melt into his warmth. Stephanie had a moment of clarity realizing what was happening and pushed him away.

"No." She said stepping back to put distance between them. "You don't get to do this. You don't get to come in here kissing me like you own me and leave me wanting what I know you're not willing to give. Please leave Ivan, because I can't do this. You know how I feel and if you are not willing to truly give this a try then we have nothing more to say to each other. We will keep our relationship strictly professional. If you can't accept that then consider this my resignation." Ivan backed away and stared into her eyes. His expression was serious as he spoke just above a whisper. He cupped her face with both his hands as he looked into her beautiful eyes.

"I can't get you out of my head Stephanie. You are consuming my thoughts and I can't make it stop, do you understand how that feels, not to be in total control? I sure as hell never had to deal with these types of feelings before. I don't know what to do but I know I don't want to lose you."

She looked into his eyes surprised at his revelation. "I'm willing to try. I can't promise I will be any good at it because this is foreign to me. All I know is I want you; I want you more than I've ever wanted anyone." He released her face, took her hands into his as he sat on the sofa, and pulled her onto his lap so that she straddled him. "Stephanie, look at me." She turned her face to meet his stare. "I want to be with you, are you willing to give me a try?"

"Yes." She replied. "More than anything." Tears formed in her eyes.

"Good, so we will give this relationship thing a try." He said and they both laughed.
Ivan's expression turned serious. "God, you are so beautiful." He whispered right before he began to kiss her again. This time she did not resist. He pulled her in tight.
"Steph, you feel so good." His hands travelled up her top caressing her breast. He began a trail of kisses down her

collarbone. He pulled her top over her head. Stephanie felt dizzy; she could feel his manhood expanding between her thighs. He pulled her face into his and kissed her so hard that she moaned. He parted his lips to receive her tongue and she happily complied. She could feel the wetness soaking her panties. She pulled away and stood.

"We can't do this." She said not so confidentially. "I mean we can, uh, but I can't do this now. Trust me, I want you just as much as I feel you want me, but I don't want to be just another lay for you. I know we decided to give this a try but I really think we should get to know each other before we sleep together." Ivan looked at her with a slight smile. He stood walked over to her grabbed her waist and pulled her into him.

"Steph, I will wait as long as it takes for you to be comfortable with us. I do want you but I can also understand your hesitation." He brushed his lips with hers, and then gave her a soft but passionate kiss. "Have dinner with me tomorrow night. We can go back to Napoli's."

She stared into his eyes. "Okay, what time?"

"I will pick you up at seven o'clock. I'm going to head out but I will see you tomorrow." He kissed her again then they walked towards the door. Stephanie closed the door behind Ivan and went up stairs to take a shower and possibly make use of the removable showerhead.

Ashley waited impatiently for Samantha. "What is taking her so long? If I weren't afraid, I would have a nervous breakdown. I would do the test by myself." She said out loud. Just then the doorbell rang. "It's about time." She said.

"Okay, I'm here. What's the emergency?" Samantha said annoyed.

"I told you I wanted you to be with me when I did the test." Ashley said impatiently.

"What test Ash? OOOOH. The test, why? Are you late? Do you think you might be pregnant?"

"I don't know, but it's show time. You know he doesn't even accept my calls anymore. This has to work, Sam I have to be pregnant or I may lose him forever. I don't know what's wrong with him anyway. I mean look at me. Why would he want some black chick when he could have this?" Ashley said while waving her hand over her body. "I do know that if that new black bitch he hired thinks she is going to steal my man she has another thing coming. You should have seen her Sam, walking around the office like she is better than everyone." Samantha looked at her delusional friend with pity. "Well, let's get this over with." Samantha said as she pointed to the bathroom. "You know how to do it don't you?" Samantha asked.

"Yeah, I'm not an idiot. I will be right back." Ashley huffed away and went into the bathroom. After a few minutes Samantha knocked on the door.

"Ash, are you okay? What does it say, Ash?"
Samantha opened the door and Ashley was on the floor crying. She handed Samantha the test stick. She looked at it and hugged her friend. "It's going to be okay, Ashley"

SATURDAY JULY 9th

Stephanie was getting ready for dinner with Ivan "Oh my god, I'm actually dating Ivan." She felt like a high school girl with her first crush. Her heart was pounding and her palms were sweaty. This was so surreal for her. It took her almost an hour to choose her outfit. She decided to wear a light brown silk chiffon halter dress. This was one of her favorite dresses. It really accented the color of her eyes and she chose a pair of high-heeled strappy sandals. This was their first official date and although they were going back to the same restaurant, it felt special because that place was special to him. Stephanie had a glass of wine to steady her nerves. She drained the glass before she realized it and poured herself another, careful to only take sips of this one. *'Why am I so anxious? It's not like we haven't had dinner together before.'* She looked at the clock. It was six fifty five. At that moment the doorbell rang. She drank the rest of her wine and walked to the door. When she opened the door all she could think was, *'Why is this obscenely gorgeous man attracted to me.'* Ivan wore a tailored navy suit with a powder blue silk tie. This man was sexy on a stick. Ivan took one look at Stephanie and she literally took his breath away. He was momentarily rendered speechless. *'What the hell is this woman doing to me?'*

"Come in. I'll be ready in a second." Stephanie said as she moved to the side so that he could come in.

"You look beautiful." Ivan said as his speech returned.

"Thank you, you don't look too bad yourself." She said smiling. "Do you want something to drink?"

"No, I'm fine."

"Okay, well I guess we can get going." They had light conversation while driving to the restaurant discussing their favorite music, movies, and books.

Ivan and Stephanie arrived at Napoli's and were seated right away; they ordered drinks and continued their conversation.

"Can I ask you something Ivan?" Stephanie said while taking another big sip of her wine. He nodded looking intently into her eyes. He couldn't get enough of looking at her. "Why me? You are an incredibly handsome rich man who could have almost any woman he wanted. What is it about me that attracted you? And we have yet to discuss the whole black and white issue, which by the way, does not bother me but I can imagine that it may cause raised eyebrows from individuals in both the business world as well as our circle of friends, who may not agree with interracial dating."

She stopped talking because she realized that she was babbling, which was a clear indication that she was nervous. She took another big gulp of her wine; it burned the back of her throat helping her to focus. *'God I have to slow down. I am really feeling this wine.'*

"Why not you Stephanie?" Ivan said not breaking eye contact. "You are an extremely beautiful and sexy woman, not to mention very intelligent. I feel a strong connection with you and I want to explore us." Just then the waiter came over to get their order.

"If you don't mind I would like to order for you." Ivan said with a slight smile

"I don't mind." Stephanie said surprised. Ivan told the waiter to have Marco make them both his special. He focused his attention back at Stephanie. "You will enjoy this, it is not on the menu but they will make it at my request." Stephanie finished her glass of wine and the waiter immediately refilled her glass.

"So where was I? Oh yes" he continued, "whether people will have a problem with our relationship really does not concern me. I have never allowed what people thought to dictate my actions. And while I have never dated an African-American woman before that did not mean I was closed to the possibility. Does the fact that I am another race concern you?"

"No." She said.

She had never dated outside her race but she was willing to give this relationship a try, because as much as she hated to admit it to herself she was falling in love with this man. She just hoped her heart would not lead her down that spiraling road of heartbreak.

"Good. So tell me something about you that I don't already know."

"What do you want to know?"

"Tell me about your family." Ivan said wanting to hear everything about her but more importantly, wanting to hear her voice. He had already run a background check on her, because he needed to be careful. He did not trust himself around this woman and he needed to know what he was dealing with.

"Well, I have a brother and sister, both older. My brother Jonathan is a principal in Atlanta, he went to Morehouse College and decided to stay there and teach. He met his wife Jennifer in college. They have two beautiful daughters. My sister Ciara is an accountant and lives in New York City. She is engaged and plans to marry in June of next year to a wonderful man named Malik. He is a Finance Attorney. My parents Robert and Karen Young are both retired and moved to Florida to be closer to my paternal grandparents. They live in a small community right outside of Miami. You have already met my best friends who are like my sisters. So, that's me. What about you?"

Ivan looked at her as he smiled thinking about his parents. "My parents are Liam and Gabriella Quinn. They...." Before Ivan could continue their food was brought out. Stephanie looked down at her plate not really recognizing what was on the plate.
Ivan explained that it was 'Seafood Coddle' "Try it; I want to know what you think. My mom made this dish for my brother and I when were younger. My mother is Italian, but she learned how to make Irish food to please my father who is Irish. They met in America and married at a young age. Both families were opposed to their union, but they were in love and wanted to be together. Eventually both

families came around. I don't get to see my mother and father as often as I would like. They moved back to Italy to care for my grandmother and when she passed away they decided to stay. My parents have only two sons, my brother Adam and me. Because they both come from large families we have a slew of cousins here in America, Italy, and Ireland and we all try to get together for the holidays and as much as we can."

They ate and settled into a light conversation, talking and sharing stories about their lives and families; midway through their meal Ivan's friend Marco joined them for a drink. He asked Stephanie if this was another work dinner. Ivan answered for her by officially introducing him to his lady. Stephanie smiled shyly as they continued their conversation with Marco. After about ten minutes Marco excused himself to check on other guests. "Please tell Isabella I asked for her and I look forward to our talks." Marco reached for Stephanie's hand and kissed it lightly.
"I will relay your message as I am sure she is looking forward to seeing you again." He shook Ivan's hand and departed.

When they stood to leave Stephanie felt a little dizzy, realizing the wine affected her more then she realized. She held on the table.

"Are you alright?" Ivan asked.

"Yes I'm fine, just had more to drink than usual." She shook off the feeling and walked towards the entrance. Ivan placed his hand on her back as they walked out. Stephanie felt a warm sensation shoot through her body from Ivan's touch. *'God this man is so sexy. I am in deep trouble.'* She thought as she listened to the Soft jazz that pumped through the speakers of Ivan's car as they rode home in silence.

Stephanie looked at Ivan with lustful eyes; she was picturing him naked on top of her, her thoughts caused moisture to build between her legs. Ivan looked over and could see her eyes darken.

"How are you feeling?" Ivan said as he reached up and glided his thumb across her cheek. She closed her eyes and leaned into his touch as her heart fluttered.

"I am so turned on right now." She whispered not really meaning for him to hear her. Ivan smiled as he took her hand, kissing the back of it while he kept his eyes on the road. They pulled in front of her building. Ivan parked and walked around to let Stephanie out of the car. The ride home really settled the alcohol in her system and she had a little trouble standing. Ivan joked about her being a lightweight when it comes to drinking and she agreed. He walked her into the apartment building and rubbed her back as they rode the elevator to her floor. As soon as they were inside her condo Stephanie closed the door and wrapped her arms around Ivan's neck, stood on the tips of her toes and began kissing him passionately. Ivan lifted Stephanie off her feet and she wrapped her legs around his waist. He immediately backed her into a nearest wall, everything was a little fuzzy, but she knew she wanted him badly. She bit his bottom lip as she began to suck on it. Ivan ran his tongue along her lips until she gladly opened her mouth to receive his tongue. The kiss was so rough and raw. Ivan held her so tight against the wall it knocked the air out of her lungs. As she inhaled to get air she was consumed by Ivan's scent and it sent her over the edge. She started to grind her body against Ivan and could feel his hardness against her heat.

"Oh my god Ivan, I want you so bad." He showered her neck with kisses and he made his way down to her breasts raising her up to get access. She could feel him sucking on her neck and she was about to lose it. The pressure building in her body, she was on the verge of coming. Ivan ran his hand up her thigh to her middle, he could feel her wetness. He moaned and stuck his middle finger into her moist center as he used his thumb to rub her clit. Grinding her body into his hand, she started panting loudly. "If you don't stop I'm going to cum...." She yelled Ivan's name as she came. "I want you now Ivan. I want to feel you inside me now." She whispered in his ear. Ivan wanted her so bad it hurt, but not like this. He carried her to the sofa straddling her on his lap. "Baby you just don't know how bad I want you." He said as he trailed kisses down her neck. She leaned back again allowing him full access. He gripped her waist and grinded his hardness in between her thighs.

"Do you feel that, Steph? How you affect me. I want nothing more than to take you right now, but when I make love to you, I want you fully conscious, I want you to remember every moment and right now you are having trouble standing." He said with a smile. Stephanie felt a little embarrassed and slightly ashamed. She moved off his lap and sat beside him. "I'm really sorry. I don't know what came over me. I usually don't drink that much." She stood up, steadied herself and walked away from the sofa. He followed her, grabbed her by her waist, and pulled her back into his chest.

"Hey baby, it's okay. I had a great time."

Stephanie really felt stupid; first she drank too much, then threw herself at Ivan. *'What the hell is wrong with me?'* She admonished herself. "I am normally not like this. I was really looking forward to seeing you and I guess I was more nervous that I thought. Thank you for a wonderful evening." She said as she turned to face him. He brushed his lips lightly over hers. She pulled out of his embrace and walked to the door giving him his cue that it was time for him to leave. Ivan kissed her softly on her lips again. "I will call you in the morning." With that Ivan walked out the door. She closed the door and headed to the bathroom to take a shower and clear her head.

As Ivan drove home he thought about his date with Stephanie and how she affected him. *'Stephanie Young, what are you doing to me?'* His phone vibrated in his pocket and he looked at the caller id: Ashley again. "Why can't you just let go?" He said in an agitated tone, sending the call to voicemail. 'Whatever she wants will have to wait.'
He thought as he redirected his thoughts back to Stephanie.

CHAPTER NINE

SUNDAY JULY 10TH

Stephanie woke up to a throbbing headache as the phone rang continuously. She looked over at the clock; it was seven a.m. "Hello." She said with more attitude then she intended.

"Well, hello to you too. Did your date go that well?" Brianna said.

"Or do you still have company?" Tara chimed in.

"Hey guys." Her voice softened.

"So, how was your first date?" Brianna asked again.

"Horrible. I got drunk, threw myself at Ivan and then got upset when he rejected me."
"What." They both said in unison.

"Let me get this straight, our best friend, who is always volunteering to be the designated driver, who never has more than two drinks, EVER, got drunk on her first date with a guy who is fine as hell and who also happens to be her boss, then tried to jump his bones? Wow Steph that sounds like one of my dates." Tara said while laughing. Still laughing Brianna said. "You have to admit that sounds like a Tara date." "Except for the rejection part, that ain't ever happened to me." Tara said proudly. "Go ahead and joke at my expense but I may have really blown this and I'm really feeling Ivan."

"Oh sweetie that man is into you. He's not going anywhere, now there has to be a good reason you got drunk, so what happened?"

"Well I had a glass of wine before we left and while we were at the restaurant I had a few more glasses. I guess my nerves got the best of me. What am I going to do? Should I call him and explain?"

"Hell no, he needs to accept you for who and what you are, drunk and all." Tara said unable to contain her laughter.

"Goodbye guys." Stephanie said ready to hang up.

"No I'm sorry Steph I couldn't resist." Tara said. Brianna spoke up. "Stephanie seriously, I think you should wait for him to call you, and he will call, then you can explain what happened and Steph, I'm sorry your first date was not the dream date you were expecting."

Brianna really wanted her friend to find love and more importantly get laid. They continued their conversation for a few more minutes.

"Hey, before we hang up you know it's your turn to choose where we go next month Steph. So what are we doing?" Brianna asked.

"I'm not sure but I do have an idea. Look, I have to go. Are we meeting today after church for brunch?" "That sounds good." Tara said. "I'm in" said Brianna. "The usual place?" "Sounds good to me." Stephanie said. "I love you guys. See you after church."
Stephanie hung up the phone not really wanting to talk anymore.

The phone rang again and Stephanie picked it up without looking at the caller id thinking it was one of her friends forgetting to tell her something "Did you remember another joke to tell at my expense?"

"I'm afraid not." A sexy low voice said at the other end.

"Ivan, I thought you were my friends calling back."

"Are you disappointed?" He said in the sexiest voice she had ever heard.

"Not at all, I'm glad you called. I wanted to apologize for last night. I am so embarrassed about what happened. I really didn't eat much yesterday and I drank more wine than I would normally do and you saw the final result." Ivan smiled to himself not wanting to comment on her statement.

"What are you doing today? I would like to give you a chance to make it up to me."

"I am meeting my friends for brunch but I am free after that."

"Good, let me make you dinner, say about six o'clock."

"That sounds like a real treat. Text me your address and I will see you at six."

"No need. I will send a car to pick you up. Be ready at six o'clock."

"Okay." Was all Stephanie could say?

"Good. See you at six." He disconnected the call. Stephanie felt rejuvenated. She hopped out of the bed and into the shower to get ready for the day.

"Sam I have tried to call him but he is not taking my calls." Ashley said. She was so angry that he was refusing her calls. "He needs to know that he is going to be a father and he can't ignore me forever. I bet he is already sleeping with that black bitch from his office. I swear I will kill that bitch before I let her have my man."

"Come on Ash you can't seriously be contemplating violence." Sam looked worried she knew her friend was not the most stable individual.

"Of course not. I'm just talking. Besides when Ivan finds out I'm having his baby he will do the right thing. You'll see we will be a family."

"What if he doesn't, what then Ash? You have to be prepared to handle him not wanting you even if you are having his baby. You need to prepare yourself for the possibility of being a single mother."

Ashley looked at her as if she were crazy. "What are you talking about, Samantha. You know Ivan. He is very responsible and he will not let his child grow up without a stable family life."

"I'm just saying you need to be prepared just in case."
"Whatever Sam. Look I have to go."

"How do you plan on letting him know about the baby if he refuses to return your calls?" Samantha questioned.

"If he won't come to me then I will go to him. I know he will be at the formal in a couple of weeks. I plan to attend. He will not ignore me in a public setting and I will tell him then." She said looking like a light bulb just went off in her head. "Now that I think about it that will be the perfect time to tell him. Hopefully he will have that man-stealing bitch with him and I can give them both the wonderful news. By that time I can hand him a report from the doctor and an ultrasound picture." She squealed happy with her plan.

Brianna, Stephanie and Tara were seated. Sonny's was their favorite place to meet after church for brunch. "So, I've decided where we are going next month for our outing."

"So what did you come up with?" Tara asked.

"I thought it would be fun for us to get dressed up and go to a formal."

"This wouldn't by any chance be the same formal that your company is involved with because Lawrence has already invited me." Tara said.
"I was invited too, by Adam." Brianna chimed in. Both Stephanie and Tara both looked at Brianna. "Adam? Since when did you start seeing Adam?" Tara asked.
"We're not..."

Before she could finish Stephanie interrupted her.
"You are such a hoe. That's who you were with when I called you that night and you were whispering." Stephanie said smiling. Tara was shocked. "Wait a minute, Uh what?" She looked at Brianna with her mouth wide open. "You and Adam? When did this happen? Okay, Miss Prissy start talking now and don't stop until we hear every juicy slutty detail."

"Tara you are so nasty." Brianna said.

"Well apparently so are you. Now spill it."

"Well, it wasn't anything planned. I mean he called me a couple of times after we were all met at the club that night but I was too busy to return his call. Then I met with a client and the meeting went later than I expected, so when I was done, I decided to stay and have dinner alone. As I was about to leave Adam and Lawrence walked in. They invited me to have a drink with them and I accepted. After about a half hour Lawrence left saying he needed to check on you Ty. Were you sick he seemed really concerned."

"No girl, that's what the good loving does, keeps them coming back for more." Tara said as she tried to hide the fact that Lawrence had become overly protective since she confided in him.

"Anyway Adam and I stayed and continued to drink. I really enjoyed his company and before I knew it he offered to drive me home but we ended up at his place instead. Let me just say AMAZING, I will never believe that stupid ass nonsense about white man's size. Adam had the right equipment and knew exactly what to do with it. God, I lost count after the third orgasm. After such a long drought, its nights like that night that could have a sista sprung. Whew!" Brianna started hand fanning herself as if she was getting heated just thinking about their night together.

"Okay, okay calm down. He's not here so rein that shit back." Tara said jokingly.

"So you and Adam are seeing each other now?" Stephanie asked.

"I didn't say that but I am open to having a friend with benefits."

"You slut, you make me proud. I never thought I would see the day when my Bri would be open to having a sex partner without all the unnecessary strings attached." Tara said as she mockingly put her hand over her heart.
"I'm not going to lie to you guys, that night was not only hot as hell, it felt comfortable. There wasn't that awkwardness afterwards. I don't know where it's headed, but I'm going to ride it until the wheels fall off." Brianna and Tara tapped their glasses as Stephanie rolled her eyes.

"I guess I'm the only voice of reason in the land of sluts."
She smiled.

"Huh, I do believe you would have been dropping those
panties on the first date if your boss didn't put the brakes
on." Tara said laughing.

"Anyway, so are we going?" Stephanie said trying to
change the subject. "Sounds like fun. I will call Adam and
let him know that I will be his date." "With benefits." Tara
added. "I already told Lawrence I would go with him."

"Good. So now that it is decided, we need to plan a day to
go shopping."
"Now, guess who has a date with an extremely sexy man
today?" Stephanie said gloating. Tara and Brianna said "I
do." In unison. They all looked at each other and laughed
so loud that the other patrons started staring.

CHAPTER TEN

Stephanie arrived home and immediately started getting ready for her date. Since they were having dinner at Ivan's house she decided to wear a strapless sundress with a pair of strappy sandals. Danny, Ivan's driver picked Stephanie up at exactly six o'clock and they arrived at Ivan's Condo at six thirty. The doorman was aware of her arrival and escorted her to the elevator, inserted a key and then pushed the button to the fortieth floor. *'So this is how the other half lives.'* She thought.

When the elevator reached the fortieth floor the door opened to the foyer of Ivan's condo and he was at the door to greet her with a glass of wine.

"Welcome to my home beautiful. You look amazing."

"Thank you." She said as she accepted the glass of wine.

"Well come in and let me show you around." Stephanie was in awe of her surroundings. "Your place is beautiful Ivan." She said while looking at everything around her.

"Is that wine okay? I can get you something stronger if you would like." She raised her eyebrow and said. "Trying to be funny, huh?" He smiled remembering yesterday's incident.

"We'll just stick to one glass of wine." He went to the bar and poured himself a glass of scotch. After showing Stephanie around, they sat on the sofa in the living room.

"So what's for dinner?"

"I actually cheated and picked up something from Napoli's."

"You really like their food." She said smiling.

"Yeah, it reminds me of home." He said shyly.

They ate their meal while having a light conversation. After dinner they stood on the patio with their drinks. "Ivan, you have an amazing view of Philly's skyline." Stephanie nursed her second glass of wine determined not to have a repeat of what happened last night. She admired the skyline, while Ivan admired her. He could not keep his eyes off of her.

"Come here." He said in a soft sexy but commanding voice. She walked over and leaned into him as he pulled her into an embrace. She wedged her body in between his legs. His scent was so intoxicating she inhaled deeply and rested her head on his chest. He rubbed her back with long gentle strokes as he rested his chin on her head.
"Steph, you feel so good." He kissed the top of her head softly. "You are so beautiful."
She looked up at him and smiled as he tucked a curl behind her ear. He looked into her amazing hazel eyes and a warm feeling radiated throughout his body. "I want you so bad it hurts, but I will give you time."

"I want you too and I think the time is right."

Ivan pulled her away from his chest and looked into her eyes. "What are you saying?"

"I'm saying I want you too. I've wanted you since the first time I saw you in the office and you touched me."

"Are you sure Steph? You don't have to rush this because of what I said. I will wait."

She looked into his eyes and saw his apprehension. She wanted this man. She had been in a constant state of arousal since meeting him. "Yes, I've never been surer about anything in my life."

His lips met hers and she felt a tingling sensation running through her body. His kiss was filled with so much passion she literally felt light headed. She could feel the moisture build between her thighs. She wanted him so badly. She could feel his hands all over her body as he continued the assault on her lips. He grabbed her ass so tight and pulled her body into his and she could feel his erection on her stomach.
'Jesus he feels huge.' Ivan lifted her up and she wrapped her legs around his waist. Ivan could not get enough of her. He had never felt this way about any other woman. What was she doing to him? The feeling was indescribable. *'Could this be Love?'* The thought of it scared him. His distracted look caused Stephanie to ask him if he was okay. He responded with a nod, he could not speak so he just pulled her into a tighter embrace, which was so tight she gasped for air and he loosened the embrace. He carried her to the bedroom, sat her on the bed and kneeled in front of her. Ivan could feel her body trembling. Stephanie was extremely nervous. No, not nervous, scared. Scared because she was giving herself to this man so soon, but she wanted him, all

of him. She had opened her heart to him and she had to trust that he would not hurt her.

"We don't have to do anything you don't want to do and if you want me to stop just say so. This is the most beautiful gift you can give and I don't take this lightly. Do you understand what I am saying, Steph? I want to be your first and your last."

"Yes. I understand."

She wrapped her arms around his neck and pulled him into a kiss. He ran his tongue along her bottom lip before pulling away; he removed her shoes and slowly ran his hands up her legs stopping just below her thighs. A shiver ran through Stephanie's body. "Stand up, baby." She did as instructed. Ivan grabbed the hem of her dress and slowly lifted it up over her head.

He moaned when he saw that she was not wearing a bra, just a white lace thong. He wanted to devour her. He was so turned on, he wanted to push her on the bed and slam his dick into her, but this was the woman he loved and wanted to marry. *Love – Marriage – Where did that come from?*

"Are you okay?" She questioned as he stood their staring at her.

"Yes. I am in awe of your beautiful body." She stood there feeling vulnerable and embarrassed, she looked way. Ivan used his index finger to bring her face back to him. "Hey, don't ever be embarrassed." His lips came down on hers and his tongue invaded her mouth, she moaned as he released her lips and trailed kisses down her neck. He stopped at her left breast, sucking her nipple and he used his right hand to tease the other nipple. Stephanie felt the pressure building up in her body. She moaned loudly as he kept up the assault on her breast, alternating back and forth with his lips. "Open your legs, baby." Stephanie did as instructed, widening her stance. Ivan used his right hand and pushed his middle finger inside her wetness as he used this thumb to massage her clit. His mouth pulled away from her nipple. "Baby, you are so wet." He said as he moved his finger in and out of her. She was so tight.

"Ivan, it feels so good. Oh, baby, I'm coming, I'm com...." She screamed his name and held onto Ivan as her whole body shook. Ivan held on to her with his left hand wrapped around her waist and her pussy pulsated around his finger. When her body calmed down he laid her on the bed and removed her thong. He got back on his knees and pulled Stephanie's body to the edge. Ivan admired her pussy. It was clean- shaven except for a patch of nicely trimmed hair in the middle. He hooked her legs over his shoulders and leaned into her center, he inhaled taking in her wonderful smell. He licked her fold with one long stroke of his tongue. Stephanie arched her back as she felt the tingling in her pussy. "You taste and smell amazing." He settled in between her legs and began to suck her clit and lick her moist lips. He trailed kisses up and down her fold; he sucked on her fold before sticking his tongue inside the center of her wetness. He started feverously tongue-fucking her as she screamed out "Yes, ohh... fuck... yes..." As his tongue moved in and out of her he used his thumb to rub her clit creating amazing friction.

"Ivan, oh my god, Ivan." Before she could say anything else her body started to shake. He placed his hand on her lower abdomen to hold her in place so that she could feel the full effect of her orgasm. When her body stopped shaking, Ivan quickly removed his clothes, grabbed a condom out of his nightstand and sheathed himself. Stephanie knew Ivan was well endowed because she had felt his thickness a few times when he was aroused, but actually seeing his size made her nervous. Her eye quickly scanned his body. His body was beautiful. Ivan could sense her nervousness as she zeroed in on his very hard erection.

"Don't worry baby. It will fit."

He helped Stephanie move to the middle of the bed and nestled his body in between her legs. Stephanie halted his progress as she sat up and placed her hands on his chest running her fingers down over his stomach.

"Your body is so beautiful Ivan." She kissed his chest before looking into his eyes. She could see the love he had for her. She nervously lay back on the bed.

"How do you feel, baby?" Ivan said hoping that she was finally relaxed.

"I feel wonderful." She could feel his manhood at her entrance as he looked into her eyes. "There is no going back, Steph, once you give me this beautiful gift it can't be returned." She nodded. He slowly penetrated her using small strokes as the tip went in and out of her, then with one swift movement his dick was totally inside of her, filling her completely, tearing the thin skin which was a clear indication that he was indeed her first.

"Argh!" she moaned. Unable to breathe momentarily. Her eyes widened, shocked at the intense pain she was feeling. Ivan held her still allowing her body to adjust to his size. Ivan felt light headed, he closed his eyes as he steadied himself. *'Shit.... oh shit, hold still and don't hurt her.'* He coached himself. Her body felt amazing. She was so tight and so warm. He wanted to stay inside her forever, but mostly he wanted to slam inside her again and again. Looking down at her brought him back to the fact that this was his baby's first time and he wanted it to be memorable for her. Stephanie's eyes were closed tightly.

"Look at me, Steph... Babe, look at me."
She opened her eyes. His soft sexy eyes stared back at her.
"You okay?" She nodded so overcome with emotions she was unable to speak. A tear ran down the side of her face and Ivan followed the tear with kisses. "I need to move baby okay." The pain started to subside and Ivan began to move slowly in and out of her.

She could feel the tingling sensation in her pussy again causing her to move with him, encouraging him to move faster. Ivan lost the last bit of control over the situation when she thrust her hips upward to meet his strokes. "That's right baby, give it to me. This. Is. Mine". He said emphasizing each word with a thrust inside her.
He moved faster and harder. He could actually feel the buildup in her body; she was on the verge of coming again. She moaned "Ivan. Ivan. Huh."
She started to shake and her inner muscles gripped his dick and he continued to pump in and out of her he thrust his hips one last time roaring "MINE!" He emptied his seed into the latex separating them. He wished for the first time

in his life that he did not have the barrier; he wanted to fill this woman, his woman, with his seed.

He whispered in her ear, "You are mine" before he collapsed on her as they both struggled to get their breathing under control. Ivan went to the bathroom to remove the condom and got back into the bed and pulled Stephanie close to his chest as she quietly slept. Ivan couldn't sleep as he replayed the events of tonight in his head. He wanted her again. He got up and headed towards the shower and allowed the three showerheads to rejuvenate his body. After getting out the shower and drying off, he heard Stephanie moving around in the bed. He ran water in the hot tub. He wanted her to soak, he was sure her body was sore. He walked into the bedroom with a towel around his waist.

"Hey you." Stephanie said softly.

"Hey yourself." He said while getting back in bed. "How are you feeling baby?"

She looked into his eyes she loved the terms of endearment he used. She lowered her head feeling a little shy. "I feel amazing, overwhelmed, sore and loved." She said while kissing him.

"Well, I have a surprise for you." He said as he picked her up and carried her into the bathroom.

"What are you doing?"

"I thought a soak in a hot tub might help with the soreness." He removed his towel as he stepped into the hot tub with Stephanie in his arms. Once submerged in the water he pulled Stephanie in between his legs. The water was soothing to Stephanie's throbbing pussy. The jets created soothing bubbles around their bodies.

"This feels amazing, thank you." She looked over her shoulder and reached up to kiss him. He started kissing her on her neck and shoulder; she could feel his erection on her back. Although she was still a little sore she wanted him again. She turned around to straddle him, placed her arms around his neck and kissed him passionately. She started grinding her body against his hardness.
"How do you feel?" "Sore, but I want you." He stood to retrieve a towel for himself and Stephanie. Ivan motioned her to the bed where they continued their love fest.

After waking up again, Stephanie looked up to see Ivan staring at her." Do you ever sleep?" She said yawning and he smiled. "What time is it anyway?" She said looking for a clock.

"It's five o'clock," he said. She sat up startled.

"I have to get home and get ready for work. I didn't mean to stay the entire night."

"It's okay. I think your boss would be okay with you taking the day off and spending it with your man." He said with a smirk.

"My boss may be okay with it but I'm not. Look Ivan, just because we took our relationship to the next level doesn't mean I am expecting special treatment. Well, except for the bedroom." She said with a smile.
"All right, but you can come in a little later."

"I'm fine. I just need to get home and get dressed." *'I need to be more like Tara and Brianna who are always prepared with their booty call overnight bag.'* She slipped on her sundress and pulled her hair back in a ponytail. She opted not to put back on the same underwear, which if she recalled correctly were still in Ivan's pants pocket. Ivan called his driver and he was waiting in the lobby for her. She retrieved her purse while Ivan walked her to the door trying to convince her to stay. "I will see you at work." She kissed him again before leaving out the door.

Stephanie arrived for work at nine thirty and Ivan was already there in his office working. Betty commented on her lateness. "Wild weekend huh?" Betty said while smiling and waiting for information on her weekend. "Not really. I just got a late start this morning."

"Well, I suggest you think of a better excuse before you walk into Mr. Quinn's office. He said he wanted to talk to you as soon as you got in."

"Thanks Betty, just let me put my things away and I will be right there."

Stephanie placed her purse in her drawer and knocked on Ivan's door. "Come." Ivan said with authority.

"You wanted to see me?" Stephanie said and peeked in the door.

"Yes. Come in. Close the door and have a seat." As she closed the door she could see Betty trying to hear their conversation. She sat in the seat directly in front of his desk. He got up walked around and sat on the corner of his desk. He pulled her between his legs into an embrace.

"How are you feeling?" He said in a low monotone voice as he kissed her neck.

"I don't think you want to start this in your office." She said and tilted her head to allow him full access to her neck. He gave her a soft and gentle kiss on the lips.

"Yeah, you're right." He whispered in her ear while smiling. "You are a screamer."
She playfully punched him on his arm.

"Did you want anything in particular; I have to get back to work because my boss is so demanding." She said teasingly.

"Nothing in particular, just this." He kissed her passionately. "Oh, there is one other thing. I am travelling to St. Bartholomew with Marco and Bella and I would like you to come. We travel their once a year for a long weekend. The first day Marco and I spend on business then we are free the rest of the weekend to enjoy the island. It's a beautiful place. You will love it".

"Sure. I would love to come and it will give me a chance to spend some time with Isabella. I really like her and I think we can be friends."

"Good. Betty will make the travel arrangements." She gave him a strange look. "Don't worry she has been warned about the confidentiality of this office."

"Okay. If you say so." She kissed him and walked out the door. He could tell she was still a little sore by the way she was walked. It wasn't real noticeable but he knew as he smiled.

Stephanie was inundated with work. The week went by so fast she almost forgot that they were leaving on Friday. Ivan had been out of the office most of the week, leaving her undistracted to complete the majority of her work. Betty called Stephanie and told her that Ivan had set up a meeting for her and she could conduct the meetings in his office.

"What's the meeting about?" She checked her computer. "I don't see the agenda on my schedule. Should I have known about this meeting?" Stephanie got nervous.

"Don't worry, Stephanie. This is not a meeting you need to prepare for. You will see. They will be here in about fifteen minutes."

"Okay." She sat back at her desk and tried to refocus on work.

"I will be right back. If the clients show up you can put them in Ivan's office." She went to the ladies room got some water trying to relax before the meeting that she knew nothing about. When she walked into the office Betty informed her that the individuals were in Ivan's office. She grabbed a notepad from her desk and walked into the office. She opened the door and was really confused. "What's going on in there, Betty?"

Betty walked in behind her and closed the door. "Well Stephanie, Mr. Quinn thought it might be nice for you to get a few things to take on your trip tomorrow. He realized that you have been working so hard, you may not have gotten a chance to prepare." There was a team of people in the room. Betty continued. "This young lady is a personal shopper from Neiman Marcus and she brought some outfits and swim suits that you can choose from and don't worry about size, I made sure they had the correct size. These two young ladies will do your manicure and pedicure." Stephanie smiled at everyone and pulled Betty to the side.

"I can't afford this Betty."

Betty asked the individuals to excuse them as she guided Stephanie out of the office.
"I meant to give this to you earlier" Betty said and handed her an envelope. The envelope contained an American Express Black card and The JPMorgan Chase Palladium card with her name on it.

"What's this? I am not comfortable with accepting this," she said while trying to give the envelope back to Betty.

"Please don't give me a hard time about this Stephanie. He wants to do something nice for you."

"Okay." She hugged Betty "Thank you for everything."

"Don't thank me. Thank Mr. Quinn."

'I plan to.' she thought.

They arrived on the Island Friday afternoon and went to one of Ivan's homes. Stephanie walked into the villa and was in awe, there was a spacious living area with slate flooring throughout and a gourmet fully equipped kitchen. In the center of the villa there was a Jacuzzi and cocktail bar. Ivan leaned down and whispered to Stephanie that they would make good use of the Jacuzzi. Stephanie looked up at him blushing. Ivan walked her back to one of the bedrooms.

"WOW." Stephanie said.

"You like it?" Ivan questioned.

"Well, duh. It's only the most beautiful place I've ever seen." Their suite was one of five king size bedrooms, each with its own bathroom, private terrace and its own home cinema system. Stephanie wrapped her arms around him and kissed him lightly. "Thank you for everything, this is amazing. I just don't know what I did to deserve an incredible man like you. I love you."

"I love you too and I'm the lucky one because you chose me." He pulled her into a tight embrace, lifting her off her feet and swung her around. He kissed her passionately as she wrapped her legs around his waist.

"We better go and see if Marc and Bella are settled because if we continue, they may not see us the rest of the night." She laughed as he released her and they walked into the living room. The outside of the villa was just as amazing, with a stunning, curved swimming pool flanked by coconut palms and decked terraces, overlooking the private beach.

Stephanie and Isabella solidified their friendship. They really enjoyed time with each other when the guys were out. The entire weekend was magical. And true to his word they made use of the Jacuzzi, the beach, the pool and everywhere else he felt like taking her. She loved every minute of it. On the plane ride home Stephanie and Isabella promised to get together soon.

The formal gala was fast approaching. Stephanie was spending most nights with Ivan. They could not get enough of each other. Ivan had to restock his supply of condoms. She loved making love to Ivan, she loved him so much. God help her, because she had fallen fast and hard. So much for guarding her heart. He had it lock, stock and barrel. It was like a whole new world was opening up to her. Ivan was a generous lover; he made sure she was satisfied in every way. He was also proud to openly reveal their relationship, but Stephanie had reservations about letting people she worked with know about their intimate relationship. Out of respect for her they kept the relationship relatively hidden for now.

SATURDAY AUGUST 20th

After a few shopping trips, Brianna, Tara, and Stephanie found gowns and were ready for the gala. Stephanie was really nervous about attending the Gala with Ivan. Everyone they worked with would now know that they were dating and she had knots in her stomach. She was going to have a glass of wine and decided against it. She opted for a glass of ginger ale instead.

After putting the final touches on her makeup she heard the door. She knew it was Ivan using the keys she had given him. He called out to her and she let him know that she would be out in a minute. She gave herself one last look in the mirror and said,"Not bad." She walked into the living room and she could tell by the look on Ivan's face that she did something right.

When Ivan saw Stephanie she literally took his breath away. She wore an elegant champagne-colored strapless mermaid-style gown with beading that sparkled against the satin. The color brought out the color of her hazel eyes.

"You look amazing." He said as he carefully pulled her into an embrace making sure not to mess up her dress. He leaned into her "I can't wait to get you out of that dress later." He whispered before kissing her neck. Stephanie had trouble speaking as she looked at the man who had stolen her heart. He looked so handsome in his tailor made tuxedo. It fit him like a glove. She still had to pinch herself; she could not believe this Adonis was her man. He could have any woman he wanted but he chose her.

"You clean up pretty well yourself." She said with a lustful look.

"Shall we go?" He said as he escorted her out the door.

The party was in full swing. The ballroom was decorated beautifully. When Ivan and Stephanie arrived many heads turned and the whispering started. As they tried to make their way into the ballroom many people were vying for Ivan's attention but his eyes stayed fixed on Stephanie.

Several men tried to talk to Ivan but he excused himself not really listening to the conversations. He placed his hand at the small of Stephanie's back and guided her through the crowd as they walked towards the bar. Everything was a little overwhelming for Stephanie but Ivan was in his element. As they got drinks Stephanie spotted her friends. They started walking towards them when someone else stopped Ivan.

"It's okay, Ivan. I'll be with Bri and Ty. I will see you in a few minutes." She turned and walked away before he could respond. He tried to concentrate on the conversation in front of him, but his eyes continued to wander toward Stephanie. He watched her from across the room as she laughed and talked with her friends.

"Gentlemen." He said sternly. "We are here to celebrate, enough talk about business please enjoy yourselves," with that he walked away and headed towards Stephanie when Ashley stopped him in his tracks.

"How are you, Ivan?" Ashley said with a smug look on her face.

"Fine. What are you doing here?" He said with anger in his voice.

"Well, I was invited, I was attending this event before we met or have you forgotten."

"Well, if you will excuse me my date is wait..." Ashley cut him off. "You never returned my calls."

"We have nothing to discuss. We're done. Now, please."

"We are not done. We will never be done."
He looked at her with disdain.

Ashley smiled as she rubbed her stomach. "You see, Ivan, we are going to be parents."

"What the hell are you talking about?" He said loud not caring whom around them heard.
She handed him the report from her doctor and smiled. "Baby, we are going to have a baby."

He grabbed her arm firmly while walking her towards the door. "I don't know what kind of game you are playing, but you are fucking with the wrong person. You show up here with this bullshit and I'm supposed to what, Ashley? Take you back with open arms. I suggest you find another sucker because that bastard you're carrying is not mine." He shoved the paper work back in her hands but she refused to take them. She started to cry. "This is your baby, Ivan I haven't been with anyone else but you in the last year. I love you baby, and you will see that this is a blessing."
Stephanie was across the ballroom when she spotted Ashley heading towards Ivan. Brianna also saw her approaching Ivan.

"Is that his former girlfriend?"

"Yeah. I didn't know she would be here."

Tara spoke up. "I suggest you go get your man and let her know the deal."

"I'm not worried. Ivan can handle her." Stephanie looked over and saw Ivan grab Ashley by the arm and escort her out the door.

"Oh shit. I better make sure everything is okay," Stephanie said while walked towards them.

Adam arrived back at the table to see the same scene and he excused himself while heading towards Ivan. "You think we should go over?" Tara asked. Lawrence answered. "No, they're adults. They can handle their business." He stroked her arm softly, "Would you like to dance?" Without waiting for her response, Lawrence took Tara's hand and they moved towards the dance floor.

When Stephanie reached Ivan and Ashley, she could tell he was angry. She had never seen him so angry. Adam walked up behind Stephanie and asked Ivan if everything was okay. They both turned to see Adam and Stephanie. Ashley looked up with tears streaming down her face and smiled making sure she had the full attention of her audience.

"Everything's fine Adam. I was just informing your brother that we are expecting a baby so you are going to be an uncle." She said not looking at Adam but glaring at Stephanie whose face suddenly drained of color. Stephanie looked at Ivan unable to believe what she had just heard.

"Enough of this bullshit." Ivan huffed as he walked over to Stephanie who looked at him totally stunned. He whispered in her ear that he was ready to leave.

"Wait, I forgot my purse and I need to say goodbye to Bri and Ty." He nodded as she walked towards her friends.

"I have to go, I will call you guys later." Stephanie said as she kiss Brianna and Tara goodbye.

"Wait Steph. What happened? Are you alright?"

"I'm fine. I will call you later." Before they could inquire further, she turned and walked towards Ivan. He pulled her into a passionate kiss leaving no doubt in the mind of everyone looking who he was with... They headed out the door.

"What the hell was that about?" Tara said not understanding what just happened.

Ivan was quiet the entire ride home. Stephanie wanted to question him. She wanted to know how this could have happened but she remained quiet. She wasn't even sure if he wanted her to come back to his condo with him. She got her answer when he headed in the direction of his home. She did not want to hit him with a barrage of all the questions that were swimming in her head so she continued to remain silent. She glided her hand over his and squeezed it lightly. He looked over at her and gave her a half smile, and turned his attention back on the road. He intertwined their fingers and slowly brought them to his mouth and kissed the back of her hand. When they walked into the condo, Ivan walked towards the bar and Stephanie laid her purse on the coffee table and walked to the bedroom to change into something more comfortable. Ivan poured himself a double scotch drained it in one gulp and headed towards the bedroom. He entered just as Stephanie was lowering her dress to the floor. He walked over to her and wrapped his arms around her waist, and slowly kissed her neck. She leaned her head to the side to give him full access. She moaned as he spun her around palming both her breast as he began to kiss and suck on her neck. He unhooked her bra and let it fall to the floor. He rubbed his lips across her erect nipple, slowly inhaling her scent. He loved the way she smelled. He ran his tongue around her nipple in a circular motion. Stephanie's body was on fire. She felt the moisture building between her legs and she wanted him inside of her now, but she could sense that he needed to do this at his own pace. Continuing the gentle assault on her body he took one nipple into his mouth, while massaging the other one with his hand. He lifted her off her gown as it pooled at her feet and carried her to the bed.

"Did I tell you how absolutely beautiful you looked tonight?" He said in a hushed tone. He loved this woman so much it hurt. He quickly undressed and grabbed a condom from the nightstand; Ivan stared into Stephanie's eyes never breaking eye contact as he wedged his body between her legs, nudging them apart. Realizing that she was still wearing a lace thong he ripped it from her body. Stephanie was slightly startled by the roughness but she was not afraid. This was Ivan, her man and she trusted him with her life. He lowered his head to her and kissed her gently rubbing his tongue along her lips. She opened her mouth giving him access. The kiss deepened as he thrust his tongue deep into her mouth. She could taste the scotch as she lost control sucking so hard she felt him moan. He battled with her for access of her tongue. The kiss was so passionate they both had to rip their lips away to breathe. Ivan placed his forehead against hers, breathing heavily.

"I love you so much." He said as he gently swiped her lips with a kiss.

He hooked both her legs with his arms as he entered her with a quick hard thrust. His thrusts were rough, rougher than he had ever been with her. She tried to keep up with him by thrusting upward as he pounded her like a man possessed. She was so turned on. She came so hard she felt like she lost control of her body. As the tremors slammed into her body she felt like she was floating. She yelled his name as she came. He looked into her eyes as he continued thrusting into her, his body stiffened and she could feel his dick pulsating in her. He let out a load growl as he climaxed. He collapsed on her trying not to put his full weight onto her. He couldn't move. He wanted to move, but he wanted to stay inside Stephanie forever. He placed small gentle kisses on her face and neck.

"I love you so much it scares me." He said breathing heavily. Once he was able to regulate his breathing he dismounted her and she instantly missed their connection. This scared her, he scared her. He completely owned her; her heart, her body and soul. He got up and went into the bathroom. She lay there watching his retreating back praying that this man would not break her heart because she didn't know if she could survive it. She turned her back to the bathroom door as she felt a tear slide down her cheek. Several minutes later he walked back into the bedroom sat on the end of the bed and placed his head in his hands.

Stephanie looked over knowing he was thinking about the situation that happened with Ashley. She crawled over to him and placed her arms around his waist allowing her bear breast to rest against his back. He finally spoke "I don't get it. I don't know what kind of game she's playing. She knows that I will demand a DNA test and if I find out it's not mine she will lose everything. Why is she doing this?"

"Are you sure it's not yours did you ever have sex with her without protection?" She asked realizing the filter from her brain to her head obviously hadn't kicked in. She waited for his response; he turned and pulled her into his lap.
"Look at me babe. I have never slept with any woman without protection including Ashley. I have always worn a condom."

"You know that they are not totally full proof."

"That's what has me worried. I can't imagine having to deal with Ashley, not to mention bring a baby into this situation."

"What are you going to do?"

"I don't know what I'm going to do about that situation, but I do know that right now I'm going to make love to the woman I love." He said as a declaration. She looked into his eyes and she could see the love.

Tears appeared in her eyes. "I love you too."

He lowered her onto the bed. "Hey? What are the tears for?" He said looking concerned.

"I don't know what the hell is wrong with me. I have never been an emotional person and I'm turning into a crybaby." She said with a smile.

Ivan kissed away the tears as he entered her again. She wrapped her legs around his waist. This time his strokes were gentle; he took his time as he entered her slowly and deliberately.

"I. Love. You." He said stroking her with each word. He continued. "This. Is. Mine. Look at me Stephanie. Do you hear me?" She opened her eyes looking into his beautiful green eyes that were now darker.

"Yes baby it's all yours." She said as she could feel the pressure building in her body again. She began to yell. "Oh....yes baby it's all yours... shit..." She yelled as she came.

Ivan quickened the pace of his strokes. He could feel her pussy milking him as he came hard into the latex wishing it were Stephanie carrying his baby and not Ashley.

SUNDAY AUGUST 21st

Ivan rose at five thirty and worked out for one hour; he showered in his exercise room and went to the bedroom to get dressed. Stephanie was waking up when he walked in the room.

"Hello beautiful. Sleep well?"

"Well, the funny thing about that, my man kept me up all night making love so while I did not get much sleep I am well rested." She said with a smile.

He leaned down and kissed her on the lips. "Adam is coming over this morning. Apparently he had a conversation with Ashley after I left and he wants to talk to me."

"Okay, I will shower, get dressed, and get out of your hair." She said smilingly.

"I never want you out of my hair, I would like you to stay, if it's not too uncomfortable for you." "No, I'm fine. I just don't want to intrude."
"You are my woman, it's impossible for you to intrude. You are a part of my life now."

"Okay I'll stay." Stephanie didn't tell him she was a little apprehensive; she wanted to be there for him. She stood and smiled at the fact that she was not ashamed to walk nude in front of her man. As she walked towards the bathroom and her stomach immediately felt queasy, she ran into the bathroom just in time to empty the contents of her stomach in the toilet.

Ivan came up behind her, "Are you are alright, baby?" He asked as he bent over to pull her hair back while grabbing a hand towel and handed it to her.

"I'm fine my stomach is just a little upset. I think it was something I ate last night. I'm fine now, let me brush my teeth and take a shower."

Adam arrived about nine o'clock. Adam hugged his brother as he entered and walked over to the sofa where Stephanie was sitting and gave her a kiss on the cheek. "How are you doing?"

"I'm good." She said while looking at Ivan.

"So what did you need to talk to me about and I hope this is not to question me about the paternity of Ashley's baby because that is an issue I will deal with in due time."

"Well, you may be out of time. Have you listened to your messages today?"

"No. Why?"

"Well, it appears that Ashley has been in contact with Mom and she is beside herself excited about having a grandchild."

"WHAT!" Ivan was seething. This side of Ivan unnerved Stephanie.

"She has no fucking idea who she's dealing with. That bitch will regret the day she got my family involved in her bullshit." Stephanie stood beside him and began to rub his back.

"Are you so sure it's not yours Ivan?" Adam asked. Ivan pulled away from Stephanie's touch and walked over to the window staring at the skyline.
"I don't know. I mean I always used protection with her. Hell, I've never slept with a woman without a condom, it doesn't make sense. I am fairly certain that while we were together we were exclusive."

"Then it appears your problems have just grown tenfold because mom is now involved. She left several messages for you and had me on the phone almost an hour wanting to get more information about the pregnancy and why you hadn't told her."

"Fuck." Ivan could not believe this was happening.

"It gets worse. Mom has summoned us to Italy and she wants you to bring Ashley with us."

Ivan immediately looked over at Stephanie who was now sitting back on the sofa visibly upset and confused. Ivan sat down on the sofa next to Stephanie and pulled her onto his lap. "I can't do that, Adam." Ivan said while looking into Stephanie's eyes and tried to gauge how she was feeling.

"I don't think you have a choice big brother. Mom is expecting a call today with the date of our arrival." Adam stood and walked towards the door.

"Look, I have to go but call me after you talk to mom."

CHAPTER ELEVEN

It was interesting to see the type of hold the matriarch of Ivan's family had over Ivan and his brother. After speaking with his mom, Ivan rearranged his plans for the following weekend so that he could fly to Italy.

Stephanie lay on the bed exhausted from another intense love making session with Ivan. He pulled her body into a spooning position as they lay in darkness.
"I want you to come with me to Italy." He whispered in her ear. "I want my Mom to meet you. She needs to meet the woman I'm in love with."

"I can't go Ivan, your mom is expecting Ashley."

"Ashley is not going and I need to explain this situation in person. My parents need to understand that you are my lady and if Ashley is having my baby then I will take care of my responsibility."

Ivan looked at Stephanie and could see fear in her eyes. He sat up and pulled her into his lap, and kissed her gently. She melted into his embrace and tried to relax.

"Yes baby. I will go with you." She said not totally sure of how she felt about this situation.

Friday August 26st

Ivan, Stephanie, and Adam boarded Ivan's private jet and flew to Italy. True to Ivan's word, Ashley did not come. There was a six-hour time difference so when they arrived in Abruzzo it was almost 11 p.m. and Ivan had a car waiting when they arrived. The ride to his parent's home took an hour. Although it was late there were several family members there to greet them when they arrived including his parents. When the trio walked into the house, Ivan's parents immediately greeted their sons with hugs. Ivan grabbed Stephanie's hand and pulled her close to him. His mother gave Stephanie a strange look and asked who she was in Italian. Adam spoke up first and said she was Ivan's assistant at work and Ivan interrupted him by saying that this was the woman in his life. Stephanie did not understand what was being said but she knew it was not good because his mother put her hand over her mouth and started yelling in Italian.

"Ivan come hai osato portare un'altra donna in casa mia quando la gravidanza fidanzata è addormentato su per le scale." (Ivan how dare you bring another woman into my house when your pregnant fiancée is asleep upstairs.)

Ivan's body stiffened and he pulled Stephanie closer to him.

He shouted. "Perché lei sente? Essa non è la mia fidanzata. Stephanie è la donna della mia vita e se nonè possibile accettare che lasceremo." (Why is she here? She is not my fiancée. Stephanie is the woman in my life and if you cannot accept that we will leave.) Ivan's mom turned her back to Ivan and Stephanie. Ivan pulled Stephanie's arm practically dragging her out of the room towards the door. Adam ran after them. "Bro don't do this, you need to stay and clear this mess up."

"I will be back tomorrow." He walked up to Adam and said barely above a whisper. "Non tornerò qui se Stephanie non viene accolto" (I will not stay here if Stephanie is not welcome.) His intention was for her not to understand what he said but she knew it concerned her. They walked out the house into a waiting car.

"Portarci in hotel Vicoria." Ivan said to the driver.

"What the hell was that about? Are you just getting around to telling your mom your dating a black woman, if so that was pretty shitty." Stephanie said believing that his mom was reacting to the fact that she was black.

"I am not having this conversation with you right now. We will talk at the hotel."

"The hell we will. We are discussing this now."

"Enough Stephanie." He yelled and startled her. "We will discuss this at the hotel."

She looked at him ready to explode but could see the pain in his face as he looked straight ahead, avoiding her stare. They arrived at the hotel twenty minutes later but Ivan's phone continued to buzz the entire ride and he refused to answer it. Once inside the suite Ivan immediately made himself a drink.

"Do you want one because I'm going to have several?" He said with a faint smile. She shook her head.

"Do you now want to explain to me what the hell just happened at your parent's home?"

Ivan took another gulp of his drink. "Let me first say that my parents are not prejudice they have taught my brother and I to treat everyone equally. So you being black was not the cause of my mother's blowup." He took another sip of his drink.

"Me bringing a mistress into her home while my fiancée with child lay upstairs in her home sleeping, now that's the problem. He said sarcastically. You see babe, it's appears that Ashley has been a busy little bitch and she has been at my parent's home for the last few days waiting for our arrival. I did not inform my parents that I was bringing my girlfriend because I thought we could clear up this situation with Ashley, introduce the love of my life to my parents and show you where I grew up. Needless to say that plan has been shot to hell."

Stephanie looked puzzled. "Why is she here? I don't understand."

"It seems she contacted my mother a few days before the gala to give her the good news about the baby." He said sarcastically. "She also asked my mother not to say anything to me about her visit because she wanted to surprise me. Oh and the best part is that she has my entire family duped into thinking that we are getting engaged." He said with a huff and drained the rest of his drink.

"You know that getting drunk is not going to make the problem go away."

"I know but it will make me forget for a little while." She took the glass out of his hand. "I know something else we can do to make you forget for a little while." She said seductively as she starting kissing him.

The next morning Ivan left the hotel early to deal with the fiasco that was unfolding at his parent's home. "Are you sure you will be okay for a couple of hours?"

"I will be fine, I may take a cab to the market place."

"No, I will send the car back and it will be at your disposal."

She put her arms around his neck. "Thank you don't worry about me just handle your business at your parents so you can come back and handle your business with me." She said smiling.

"I've created a sexual demon." He said as he brushed his lips against hers.

"I'll be back soon." He said and smacked her on the butt then left the room.

Stephanie showered, ate breakfast and headed downstairs to a waiting car.
A girl could get use to this.' She smiled as she slid into the backseat of the car.

"Where would you like to go madam?" The chauffeur asked.

"I would like to go to the market place."

"Very good Madam."

Stephanie spent the next couple of hours buying souvenirs for everyone. The prices were so reasonable that she used euro instead of the credit cards Ivan gave her. After she shopped Stephanie stopped at a small café, and sat at table outside to enjoy the weather and scenery, while she drank her coffee and ate her scone.

As Stephanie watched the people walking by she noticed two familiar faces. It was Ivan's mom and Ashley, they were apparently shopping. Ashley spotted her and gave her a faint smile. She said something to Ivan's mother who looked in Stephanie's direction. Ashley pretended to be upset and Ivan's mom comforted her while signaling her to a waiting car. Stephanie could not believe the scene that just unfolded in front of her.

'What a goddamn actress. Oh, this bitch got game, but she will not get my man.' Stephanie thought as she finished her coffee and headed back to the hotel. Stephanie waited hours for Ivan, she tried his cell phone but it went straight to voicemail.

"This is bullshit, how do you leave me in a hotel in a foreign country and don't even call to check in." Stephanie was fuming and finally at six o'clock she decided to have dinner without him. She grabbed her purse and there was a knock at the door. She swung the door open, "It's about time do you..." She stopped mid sentence staring at Adam and not Ivan. "What's wrong Adam, is Ivan okay? I have not heard from him since this morning." He walked into the room and sat on the sofa.

"He's fine Steph, calm down. He had to fly Ashley to the hospital in Rome. She came back from the shopping trip with mom; she was visibly upset and started developing pains in her stomach. Ivan didn't want to take any chances so he flew to Rome with her. I just heard from him, the doctors said she is fine but they want to keep her

overnight for observation." "Unbelievable, he couldn't tell me himself."
Adam looked at Stephanie with compassion.

"Have you eaten? Let me take you to dinner. I know a really great restaurant not far from here."

"Okay lets go, I was going stir crazy in this room." They went to a quaint restaurant near the market place she visited earlier. They were seated and ordered their meal.
"So what's really going on Adam? I feel like I'm an intruder in this situation."

"Steph, you have to understand that my parents are very old fashioned in their beliefs. The moment my mother found out that Ashley was pregnant with Ivan's child, she was expecting him to do the right thing by marrying her."

"We don't even know if it's his baby."

"I think Ivan's convinced. This is extremely difficult for him to go against our mother. Never in our lives have we gone against anything our parents have requested of us. So for him to take a stand against my parents wishes is a big deal, bigger than you can imagine. This is not an easy situation."

"So what do you suggest Adam that I give up and go back to the states?"

"Of course not, I want to let you know that if you and Ivan are determined to stay together, you need to be prepared for the fallout of your decision. I really like you and Ivan together, I know my brother loves you but sometimes when things are set in motion there is no going back."

"So, you think Ivan will leave me and marry Ashley."

"No not at all, I think that he will stay with you and it will cause a major rift between my parents and Ivan. Ivan is the strongest man I know but when it comes to our parents he always felt the need to please them even if it was doing something he felt strongly against."

"Well how can I really compete with that?"

Adam was silent. Their meal was served and they ate in silence. Trying to change the subject Stephanie asked Adam how things were going between him and Bri. He talked about wanting more of a relationship but Brianna was against it. They also talked about this beautiful small town and Adam promised to show Stephanie around tomorrow if Ivan was still tied up.

Ivan and his parents were sitting in the living room having a heated discussion about Ashley, Stephanie, and the baby. Ivan's parents were adamant that he marry Ashley as to not disgrace the family by having a baby out of wedlock.
"This is not the 1900s, people have babies all the time without being married and tell me mother, how is it that I'm disgracing this family. I employ most of them and pay them handsomely. I don't need or want their approval. I only need you and papa to understand why I can't marry her. I will take care of my responsibility by providing for Ashley and the baby, but I don't love her and I will not marry her. I am in love with Stephanie and when I am ready to marry, she is the one I will ask."

His mother left the room too upset to speak. His father looked at him disappointed and in Italian said. "We raised you to be a good man and while your mother and I do not agree with your decision I will respect it. Come have a drink with your papa."

His father was a man of few words and the fact that he would respect his decision was good enough for Ivan. Ashley was in another part of the house; she excused herself to use the bathroom and stood outside the door where Ivan and his parents were talking. She overheard the conversation and was devastated.

How could he even consider marrying the black whore? Well at least she had an ally in his mother and she was going to use it to her advantage.
'Hell will freeze over before I let her marry my man and father of my baby.' She thought to herself. When she heard his mother exit the room she hurried back to the kitchen where the other women were gathered.

Adam dropped Stephanie off at the hotel before returning to his parent's home. There were a few messages left at the hotel for Stephanie from Ivan saying he would see her in the morning. After a restless night Stephanie knew what she had to do. When she woke up she called the airport, scheduled a flight to the states, and packed.

Stephanie arrived home late Sunday evening. She dropped her bags on the floor and headed towards her bedroom. Stephanie removed her clothes walked into her shower and turned the water on she didn't even flinch at the initial spray of cold water. She stood in the shower and the tears rolled down her cheeks, as she sobbed uncontrollably. She became nauseous and ran out of the shower, just making it to the toilet bowl before she emptied the contents of her stomach. She sat on the floor naked, holding on to the bowl as she cried.

MONDAY, AUGUST 29th

Stephanie arrived at work to a barrage of questions from Betty. She rearranged Ivan and Stephanie's schedule so that they could make the trip together. Betty was surprised to see her back so early. Stephanie could not answer her questions; she was still too upset to deal with that situation. She just wanted to keep busy and the best way to do that was to come to work.

"Ivan and Adam are still in Italy. I cut my trip short and I really need to catch up on my work." Betty looked confused but sat back at her desk. Around three o'clock Betty buzzed Stephanie to tell her she had a call on line two.

"Quinn Corporation Stephanie Young speaking. There was silence but she could hear breathing. "Hello." She said

"Why the hell did you leave?"

"I don't want to talk about this now Ivan. I don't want everyone in the office knowing our business."

"It's my fucking office, I don't give a shit about what MY employees think." Ivan said in a low angry tone.

"Ivan I will call you when I get home, I can't do this now."

"Fine." He said then hung up.

Stephanie got home fixed dinner and took a shower. She did not have the energy to talk to Ivan right now. *'I will take a nap and call him later.'* Stephanie didn't wake up until the next morning. She had several missed calls from Ivan. *'Shit, he must really be angry.'* She tried to call him but his phone went to voice mail. I guess I will have to face the music at work. Stephanie arrived at the office refreshed and ready to face what was to come. She noticed Ivan's door open as she walked to her desk. She put her purse away and began to work on the assignments on her desk.

Ivan came out of his office and immediately knew Stephanie was there. He could smell her lovely scent. He looked over at her desk but was too angry to address her there. He had to prepare for an important meeting. Stephanie would have to wait until later. He left the office without speaking to her. Her heart sank *'You can do this girl be strong.'* Stephanie was so busy that she forgot to take lunch. At five o'clock Stephanie headed for the door glad that she avoided Ivan today. "Goodnight Betty, I will see you in the morning." And she walked out of the door Ivan grabbed her arm and swung her around. "We need to talk." He released her arm and turned to walk back to his office. She followed him into his office and he closed the door. Still so angry it was hard for him to speak.

"What was that little stunt you pulled in Italy?" He said talking through his teeth.

178

"Stunt, stunt, the stunt was you leaving me in a hotel in a foreign country alone while you traveled around with your baby mama!" She yelled back.

"Don't be ridiculous, she needed medical attention. I was not going to let anything happen to my baby." "My baby? Oh now you're sure it's your baby, you know what..." She put her hand up in the air. "I'm done. I can't do this because that conniving heifer will do anything to be with you including sabotaging our relationship. She already has your mom hating me."

"Stephanie stop acting like a fucking child, yes, I do believe the baby she is carrying is mine but that does not mean we can't be together."

"Now I'm a fucking child? You know what Ivan I'm done. Have a good life with your psycho baby mama." She turned to walk away but Ivan grabbed her by the arm and swung her around holding her in a tight embrace.

"Ivan, let me go before I slap the shit out of you." She said as the tears started streaming down her face. He held her as she struggled to get free. She pulled away from him and tried to slap him but he caught her hand. He picked her up and placed her on the sofa, climbed on top of her, grabbed her by her neck, and pulled her into a kiss. She tried to resist but was unable. She felt his erection on her thigh. Her body felt like it was on fire. She felt the moisture building between her legs. Right at that moment, she hated that her body responded to his touch. He reached under her skirt and ripped her panties off. She squirmed under him and he inserted his finger into her heat. "You are so wet." He breathed into her ear.

She arched her back and moaned, angry that her body her body would betray her so easily. She knew it belonged to him. He then inserted another finger and thrust them in and out of her.

"Please Ivan stop, someone might come in." She said with tears in her eyes. He brought his lips back down on hers. She loved this man, she loved his body and God help her she was hopeless to his advances.

She felt the onslaught of an orgasm. Just as she was about to yell, he muffled her screams with his mouth. He flipped her around so that she was on her knees bent over the sofa. He took a condom out of his pocket and sheathed himself. He grabbed her hips and slammed his dick into her from behind. She bit her bottom lip to keep from screaming. He felt so good and she was angry with herself for enjoying it so much, she was angry with him damn it. His thrusts quickened and she backed into his erection meeting every thrust. He could feel her pulsating around him as she was about to come again. Her orgasm exploded in her body as she heard a low grunt from Ivan as his body stiffened. They both collapsed on the floor. Once their breathing returned to normal, Ivan turned Stephanie's body to face him. He cupped her face, and looked into her eyes as he spoke.

"I love you baby. It's going to be challenging but we can make this work, I know we can." He leaned over and kissed her as he laid his forehead against hers. "It exerts too much energy to be angry with you and I don't want to fight. Let's go home. I need you in my bed, under me." He kissed her again and she could feel his need because she had it too. They fixed their clothes, Ivan grabbed his jacket and they headed to his condo.

Over the next several weeks, Ivan tried really hard to keep their relationship as normal as possible but he was being pulled in several different directions and Ashley was demanding more of his time. Something had to give and she had a feeling it was going to be her. The stress of the entire situation caused her to eat more and she started putting on weight. She really needed to get her life together.

CHAPTER TWELVE

FRIDAY SEPTEMBER 23rd

They were suppose to have dinner together on Friday evening but as usual something was wrong with Ashley and he needed to check on her. He got to Stephanie's house about 11 p.m. He looked tired as he sat on the sofa "Stephanie, we need to talk." Stephanie sat next to him and he pulled her into his lap. He inhaled deeply. "You smell so good, God I love you so much." He said so low she did not think it was meant for her to hear.

"I love you too baby."

He kissed her on her lips softly. "I can't do this anymore. I love you so much but I can't do this."

"You can't do what? US?" She questioned and looked into his eyes.

"Yes, it's not fair to you, I can't give you the attention you deserve. We need to end this." She jumped up.

"What are you talking about? You are the one who said that it would be challenging, but we could work through it. We can work through this baby, please don't do this, don't do this to us." She grabbed his face and looked into his eyes. The tears streamed down her face.

'I need to make a clean break and get out of here, otherwise I'm going to lose my nerve.' He couldn't stand seeing her hurt so badly. He needed to leave while he still had a shred of courage. He stood to leave and she grabbed him around his waist and held onto him tight.

"No baby, don't do this. Let's just go to bed and we can work this out in the morning, you look so tired." If she only knew, he was tired and his heart was breaking in a million pieces. The last thing he wanted to do was break her heart, but he gave his word and his word was his bond, and he would have to live with the consequences.
He pulled out of her embrace and walked towards the door.

"Look, let's not make this harder than it already is. We are over Stephanie."

She was stunned. Ivan felt her body shake and wanted to hold her, but he knew that would confuse the situation. "What are you doing Ivan, we can work this out, I don't need a lot of time." She wrapped her arms around his neck and started kissing him. "Don't do this baby, I need you."
He pulled her hands from his neck. He was so cold. How could he be so cold if he loved her? "You can still stay with the company, but you will be transferred to a different office." Stephanie's head was spinning. She felt like she was in a bad dream.

"Please I need you. Don't do this." She labored over every word as she sobbed uncontrollably.

"Goodbye Stephanie."

Stephanie grabbed his jacket and yelled. "Why are you doing this Ivan, I gave you every part of me and this is how you treat me, you rip my heart out." He yanked her away and her body slumped to the floor as she continued to cry, his heart sank, he knew exactly what she meant because his heart was also ripping. "Take care of yourself Stephanie." Was the last thing he said to her before walking out the door and out of her life.

"Fuck you Ivan, I hate you, you hear me I hate you." She screamed through the door.
He leaned against her outside door and willed himself to move as he tried to compose himself. Ivan got in his car placed his head on the steering wheel and allowed the tears to fall. He never remembered shedding one tear in his adult life, but he sat there unable to control his emotions. He allowed others in his life to dictate his fate, now he would have to suffer the consequences.

SEPTEMBER 26th

Stephanie tried to pull it together. She cried so much over the weekend that she made herself sick. When she arrived at Ivan's office Betty had her stuff boxed up and showed her to her new office. Betty gave her a gentle hug and told her to call if she needed anything. She could see tears in Betty's eyes.

"Don't Betty, if you start it is going to make me start and I won't be able to stop."
Betty wiped her tears gave Stephanie a smile and walked away.

Stephanie settled into her new position. She was working with one of the managing directors, Peter Cummings. He was an older gentleman who was married with two kids in college. The workload was not nearly as demanding as Ivan's office, but it was the same pay and it kept her busy.

OCTOBER 6th

The best part of her new job was that it was on a different floor and she did not run into Ivan. She had been working in the new office for almost two weeks and was adjusting well. Stephanie had also managed to avoid Brianna and Tara. She did not want to talk about the breakup. How could she explain something that she did not understand herself? She left them a couple messages, making sure she called when she knew they wouldn't answer. She tried to leave upbeat messages so they wouldn't get suspicious. Just thinking about him caused her heart to hurt. She could not allow herself to think about him so she redirected her attention back to her work.

Mr. Cummings came out of his office. "Stephanie I need you to check your calendar and see if you are available to attend a meeting with me on October 12 ."

"Sure thing Mr. Cummings." "Peter, please call me Peter."

"Okay Peter." She pulled out her calendar and realized something disturbing. "Shit." She looked at the calendar again. "No, this can't be happening." She whispered.

"Is everything okay Stephanie?" Peter asked.

"Yes, I'm.....uh I'm fine I just realized that I have a doctor's appointment that I forgot about, but yes I am available to attend the meeting."

"Good now if you're not too late, go to your appointment."

"Thank you Peter, if I leave now I can just make it." Stephanie quickly grabbed her purse and headed out the door. As she rushed onto the elevator she did not notice Ivan and Ashley. Ivan was looking down at his phone, answering emails, of course Ashley noticed her right away and seized the opportunity.

"Ivan when we leave the doctor's office can we go by that baby boutique we saw yesterday, they have the cutest little clothes in the window."

Ivan inhaled deeply trying to calm his nerves. When he inhaled he could smell that wonderful scent that he had missed over the past month. He looked up to see the back of Stephanie's head. His heart instantly ached and his breathing and heart rate rose. Ivan did not acknowledge Ashley's silly question because he knew she was saying it for Stephanie's benefit. Stephanie tried to regulate her breathing but she was having a hard time catching her breath. She needed to get off the elevator. When they reached the garage level Stephanie practically ran off the elevator as she walked towards her car she felt a soft tug on her arm.

"Are you okay Steph?" Ivan said in a soft voice that melted her heart. She yanked her arm away.

"I'm fine. Shouldn't you be tending to your baby mama?" She said with venom.

She heard him say "I'm sorry" as she got in her car. She sat there for a few minutes while the tears streamed down her face.

"No, God please don't let it be." She headed to the drugstore, brought three pregnancy tests and headed home.

Stephanie sat on the toilet and cried as three pregnancy tests stared back at her all showing the plus sign. Her phone rang and she picked it up without looking at the caller id. "Hello." She said as her voice started cracking and he could hear the pain in her voice. "I just wanted to make sure you were okay you did not look well early."
The tears started to flow again. "How do you expect me to feel Ivan, huh you ripped my heart to shreds and then threw it back in my face before walking out of my life. You know what, no I'm not fine, but I will be. Goodbye Ivan." She ended the call and slammed it against the wall. It shattered into pieces; she did not have the energy to argue with Ivan. She knew their relationship was over and all she wanted to do was cry herself to sleep. The faster her heart mended the better she would be. She ignored the fact that her phone was in pieces. A few seconds later her house phone rang, she walked into the living room, ripped the cord from the wall and threw it in
the trash. She headed back to her bedroom and climbed into bed. She realized that no one would be able to contact her but she just wanted to sleep. Stephanie woke up the next morning sick to her stomach. This emotional shit was

not healthy for her or the baby. She decided to call in sick and stay in the bed the rest of the day. She realized that she couldn't call because she broke her phones. Not having the energy to go out and get a new phone, she climbed back into bed.

The days turned into nights, then into days again, she still had no desire to talk to anyone including her best friends. It hurt so bad she just wanted to sleep. She got up to go to the bathroom and saw Ivan's robe hanging on the door. The tears started again. On her way back to bed she grabbed his robe and wrapped it around her she could smell his scent as she laid back in the bed and went to sleep. When she woke up again she forgot what day it was. She needed to eat something, she went to the kitchen and made a sandwich and got back in bed. She ate the sandwich and went back to sleep.

OCTOBER 12th

Brianna called Tara. "Hey Ty have you heard from Steph?"

"No, but what's new, lately she's so busy up Ivan's ass that she doesn't have time for us."

"Whatever." Brianna said agitated. "Adam called me today and asked me if Stephanie was okay because she had not been to work in a week and she did not call. I told him we've all been so busy we haven't seen each other in a few weeks. I've been playing phone tag with Stephanie for the last week, when I asked him why, he told me that Ivan broke up with Steph a few weeks ago. Ivan has been trying to call to check on her but she won't answer her phone". "What, why is he just telling you, he should have told you when it first happened." Tara was angry.

"Yeah, but she's our girl, we should have checked on her sooner.

"I'm on my way to her house now." Tara said with worry in her voice.

"I'll meet you there do you have your keys for her apartment."

"I'm getting them now, see you there." Brianna and Tara met in the lobby of her building. "I've tried to call her phone but it keeps going to voicemail." Brianna stated to Tara as they headed for the elevators.

They walked through her apartment calling her name. They found Stephanie in bed sleeping, looking disheveled.

"What the fuck." Tara whispered.

They walked over to the bed Brianna looked at the way her friend looked and it brought tears to her eyes, she shook Stephanie lightly. "Sweetie wake up." Stephanie look up startled at first but realized it was her friends and she started crying again.
Brianna pulled her into a hug.

"It's okay Steph we're here."

When she stopped crying Tara said, "No offense, but you stink baby girl."

Stephanie laughed for the first time in a couple of weeks but then started crying again.

"Let's go baby girl we have to get you in the shower." Tara stayed with her while she showered and changed into clean clothes. Brianna made her some soup and they all sat in the dining room eating in silence. Stephanie was the first to speak.

"I didn't guard my heart. I didn't guard my heart and he stole it and I don't know how to get it back." She said just above a whisper as the tears rolled down her face. Stephanie explained everything that transpired over the last few weeks, including their devastating breakup.

"So that's it, you're just going to let it go without a fight. You are just going to hand your man over to her?" Tara said as she was unable to stop her own tears from falling at her friend's pain.

"I don't know how to tell you the worst part of this entire mess." Stephanie said as she started to sob unable to get her breath.

"What is it sweetie?" Brianna asked in a panic.

"I'm pregnant."
They both looked at her in total shock. Brianna walked over to her and pulled her into an embrace and Stephanie stayed seated. Tara sat on the floor and laid her head in Stephanie's lap as all three women cried. Tara was the first

to speak. "I just have to ask one question. "Has he never heard of condoms?" They all started to laugh.

"We always used condoms. That's what's really crazy about this situation. Before we broke up Ivan swore to me he never sleep with Ashley without a condom and that's why he couldn't understand how she got pregnant."

"So now you both are pregnant and he chose her?" Brianna said seething.

"No Bri, he doesn't know I'm pregnant."

"So you need to tell him." Tara said. "Unless you don't plan on keeping the baby." They both stared at Stephanie.

"I could never kill my baby Ty." Stephanie said while putting her hand over her flat stomach. Brianna and Tara breathed a sigh of relief.

"Then you need to tell him Stephanie. You should not go through parenthood by yourself." Brianna said.

"I can't deal with that right now, I'm just coming to grips with this pregnancy."
They continued to talk into the night. They stayed the night with Stephanie and in the morning they all went to breakfast. As Stephanie sat in the restaurant she was feeling better about her situation. They were enjoying their food and conversation when a familiar male figure walked over to the table. "Hello ladies." Mark Parker said while only looking at Stephanie.

"Hello Mark." Brianna and Stephanie said in unison.

191

Tara just glared at him. "How are you Stephanie?"

"I'm good and you?"

"I am better now that I've seen you, you look amazing. I have tried to get in touch with you but was unable since you changed your number." Mark said in a very sexy voice.

"That should have been a hint." Tara said as Stephanie shot her the evil eye. Mark ignored the comment and continued his conversation with Stephanie.

"Stephanie I would like to see you, maybe we can go out to dinner and discuss some unresolved issues."

"That's not necessary it's a dead issue as far as I'm concerned." Stephanie said not wanting to go down that road.

"I would like the opportunity to talk to you, I felt like we didn't have closure."
There was an uncomfortable silence for about five seconds and Mark spoke again.
"Here's my number if you decide you want to talk. It was really good seeing you Stephanie, ladies." He said acknowledging them before turning on his heels and leaving.

"I will say this for the brother, he is still fine as ever." Tara said. They all giggled and went back to their conversation.

CHAPTER THIRTEEN

OCTOBER 24th

Stephanie resigned her position at Quinn Corporation and Brianna was able to find her another temp job. It was not as exciting as her old job but at least she did not have to run into Ivan and his drama. After a few weeks of working at her new job she fell into a routine. The morning sickness had subsided and she had decided to tell Ivan about the pregnancy and let the chips fall where they may. Adam came into Ivan's office and closed the door. "Have you looked at the newspaper today?"

Ivan looked up from what he was reading. "No should I have?"

"Yes it seems that your engagement to Ashley is the top story in the entertainment section."
Ivan snatched the paper out of Adam's hand. "I am so fucking tired of her antics. I don't know what I'm going to do, because of mama I agreed to marry this person I can't stand to be in the same room with. I don't think I can go through with it." Ivan stood and walked over to the window. "You know there is not a day that goes by that I don't think about her. God I miss her so much it hurts." Adam didn't have to ask who he was talking about he knew it was Stephanie. Adam just listened, he knew his brother was hurting but when their mother confided in them that she was diagnosed with cancer and her only wish was to make sure her grandchild did not enter the world a

bastard. He agreed to marry Ashley and give the baby their family name.

"Hey bro, let's go out for drinks my treat." Ivan agreed to meet him after he was done.

So I see your engagement made its way to the newspaper." Samantha said to her best friend.

"Yeah, I guess good news is hard to keep secret."

"So how is everything going between you and Ivan?"

"It couldn't be better. The best part was the mom finding out she had cancer. I was able to get her to use that to force Ivan into marrying me. His mom is a real pushover, but really sweet."

"I don't understand Ash, How?"
"Well I called his mother a couple of times a week to keep her updated on her grandchild. There hadn't really been anything new to talk about but I was able to keep tabs on Ivan. When she confided in me about her cancer scare I told her that Ivan loved her so much and would do anything to make her happy including marrying the mother of her grandchild. That's all I needed to say and she took the idea and ran with it." Samantha shook her head.

"How can you use the fact that his mother is dying for your benefit."

Ashley waved her hand in the air dismissively. "Oh please, his mother is more manipulative than I am. She had a cancer scare, the lump was benign but she did not tell Ivan that because she wants us to get married."

"This is a dangerous game your playing Ash and someone is definitely going to get hurt. I just hope for your sake it's not you."

"Stop worrying, everything is perfect and speaking of perfect look at my baby bump." She pulled up her shirt to reveal her protruding stomach.

"Has Ivan asked you to move in with him?"

"No, he has me in another condo across town, but that's going to change as soon as I tell him that the doctor doesn't want me staying by myself because of the complications I've been having."

"And what complications are they Ash?"

"Whatever I want them to be." Ashley said with anger in her voice. She was bored with talking to Samantha and she had shopping to do. "I will call you later Sam I have things to do." She left the office in a huff.

NOVEMBER 1st

Stephanie woke up in a good mood it was the first time in weeks Ivan was not the first thing she thought about when she woke up. She was having an ultrasound today and would get a more accurate date of the baby's arrival. Brianna and Tara both took time off from work to go with her. They all met at the office around the same time. "Stephanie Young." The nurse announced and they all rose. "Which one is Stephanie?" She raised her hand. "Okay you come with me and once you are settled I will come back for you two." The nurse said with a smile. They were all in the room waiting for the doctor. Dr. Sullivan came in.

"Hello ladies, I see you have a lot of support Stephanie." She smiled at the doctor.

"So let's see what's going on." She lifted the paper gown and squeezed jelly on Stephanie's stomach. She placed the Doppler on the gel and moved it around giving the screen a strange look. Stephanie looked at her friends worried. Brianna asked. "Is everything okay?"

"Yes just one minute." The doctor continued to move the Doppler around.
"Stephanie it appears you are having twins."

"What?" Stephanie said in disbelief.

Tears rolled down Brianna's face while Tara held her hand over her mouth. The doctor turned the machine up so that they could listen to the babies' heartbeats. A tear rolled down Stephanie's cheek, Stephanie got dressed and met the doctor in her office. She gave Stephanie another prescription for more vitamins, talked to her about what to expect with multiple births and then she told her that her due date was April 28th. The doctor gave her ultrasound pictures of the babies and the ladies went to lunch to celebrate.

"I can't believe this, twins. Steph, when are you going to tell Ivan? After what was printed in the paper today you better tell him sooner than later." Tara said as Brianna glared at her.

"What, she was going to see it anyway." Tara tried to state innocently.

"See what?" Stephanie asked.

"Sweetie, there was an article in the paper today announcing Ivan's engagement to Ashley." Brianna said softly.

Stephanie looked at them both stunned. She knew her and Ivan were over but she didn't think he would be so fast at moving on.

"Excuse me." She left the table and went to the bathroom.

"Should we go with her?" Tara asked.

"No, give her a minute."

Stephanie tried to steady her breathing. 'Calm down you have to think about the two precious miracles you are carrying.' She said to herself. Well if he was moving on then so was she. She inhaled deeply and returned to the table.

"You okay baby girl."

"Yeah, I will be."

They ate lunch and Tara commented on Stephanie's weight gain. Brianna and Stephanie looked at her and they both said. "Go to hell."
They all laughed.

After lunch Stephanie went back to her apartment alone. She sat for an hour staring at the engagement announcement in the paper.
She was going through her purse looking for something when she came across Mark's card she thought about it then dialed his number. They arranged to have dinner that evening; she was starting to have a hard time fitting into her clothes. Stephanie decided to wear a brown wrap-a-round dress with brown heels.
She looked good and felt good and she really needed to get out of the house. Mark picked her up promptly at seven o'clock. They decided to go to Serefine's restaurant. Although it was an Italian restaurant, she knew it was not a place that Ivan would frequent. Mark looked handsome as ever. He wore a navy suit that fit his body like a glove and he smelled so good. Yes, this was just what she needed a night on the town with someone who was good company but had no desire to go back down a romantic rode with. After they were seated Mark said. "So I have to say I was pleasantly surprised when you called."

"You thought we had some unresolved issues and to be honest I needed a night out so I thought we could both help each other out."

"It sounds good to me." The waiter came over. "Can I start you off with a drink?"

"I'll have a gin and tonic."

"And for you Miss?" The waiter said and directed his attention to Stephanie. "I'll have a glass of apple juice."

"Very good," and with that he left to retrieve their drinks.

"Steph I know you aren't much of a drinker but I do know you drink something a little stronger than apple juice."

She looked in his eyes and decided to tell him the truth. "Mark I am drinking apple juice because I am expecting."

He looked at her strange. "Expecting what?"

"Expecting a baby, actually babies I just found out today that I'm having twins."

Mark was stunned, so stunned that it took him a few seconds gather himself.

"I don't understand, if you are in a relationship why did you agree to meet me?"

"Well, I didn't think you were looking to start up a relationship again. I thought this was about closure, obviously I was mistaken." She stood to leave. "It was good seeing you again Mark."

"Wait Steph, please don't leave, I want you to stay. I want to hear how your life has been going, I didn't not mean to upset you." Stephanie sat back down.

"Thank you." Mark said as the waiter came back with their drinks.

"Son of a Bitch, I don't believe it, is that Stephanie over there?" Adam and Lawrence turned around. "Awh Hell." Adam whispered towards Lawrence. "You ready to run interference?"

"Why is there always trouble when I go out with the Quinn brothers?" Before they could react Ivan was heading towards the table. Adam and Lawrence were close on his heels. "Good evening Stephanie."
She heard the familiar voice that still sent shivers up her spine. Mark looked over at Stephanie then at Ivan. Mark could see she was visibly shaken.

"Are you okay Steph?" Mark said as he touched her hand.

"Yes I'm fine." She said softly.

She stared at Mark and introduced Ivan without turning to look at him. "Mark this is Ivan Quinn my former boss." Just as she was done with the introduction Adam and Lawrence appeared. Mark was starting to feel uneasy with the situation and if they were making Stephanie uncomfortable then they needed to leave. Mark stood. Adam walked over to Stephanie and kissed her on the cheek.

"Hey Steph, how are you?" He reached his hand out to shake Mark's hand

"Hi I'm Adam Quinn, friend and former boss of Stephanie." As Adam introduced himself, Lawrence also kissed her on the cheek and also introduced himself to Mark. Mark started to ask them to join them and decided against it. He did not like the way Ivan was staring at Stephanie; he was definitely making her uncomfortable.

"Is there a problem man?" Mark addressed Ivan. Ivan was having a difficult time keeping his anger under control. Stephanie refused to look at Ivan although she could feel his eyes burning into her skin.

"I don't know, is there a problem Steph?" Ivan said seething and talking through his teeth. Stephanie could not believe him, he dumped her, he broke her heart and he had the nerve to stand hear like he was owed an explanation. She turned to him ready to spit fire.
"No Ivan there's no problem. You will NEVER have this problem again. Oh and congratulations on your engagement you two truly deserve each other."

Mark could see a tear in her eye and moved to stand in front of Stephanie, blocking Ivan's view of her. He leaned into Ivan, looked him in the eye and said.

"You need to back away from her, you are making her uncomfortable." Ivan took his eyes off of Stephanie long enough to stare Mark down.

"If you don't back up I will take it as a threat to her and if I even think you are a threat to her, I will be forced to beat your ass."

"What.... fuck you!" Ivan yelled but before he could say or do anything else Adam and Lawrence got between the two men and forcibly ushered Ivan out of the restaurant.

"Are you okay Steph? Do you want to leave?"

"No, just give me a minute." She took a sip of her apple juice and he could see her hands trembling. She smiled "I'm fine."

"Does he know?"

"What?"

"Does he know you are having his babies?" She looked at him and said "no" softly.

"You want to talk about it?"

"Yes, but not here."

"We can get dinner to go."

"Come on Ivan, your making a scene" Adam said.

"I don't give a fuck, did you see him disrespect me." Ivan yelled.
"You disrespected his date Ivan, what did you expect him to do hand her over to you. Get a fucking grip because this shit isn't cool. You left her broken hearted remember, don't get mad because she is finally picking up the pieces and moving on with her life." Lawrence shouted.
Adam had never seen his brother out of control.

"Fuck both of you."
"Yeah yeah, now let's go find another place to get you drunk because I'm pretty sure they're not going to let us

back in there." Lawrence said as he patted Ivan on the back.

The three men ended up at Napoli's, they sat and drank. They all got drunk. Marco looked over at them and decided to join them. "Can I drink or am I the designated driver?" Marco said with a smirk.

"No, Danny's waiting outside for us."
Marco motioned the waiter to bring him a drink. They all sat solemnly at the booth.
Marco spoke up. "So, who lost their puppy?" Lawrence and Adam pointed at Ivan. "Huh... I see." Marco said.
"I don't know what I'm going to do, this shit is making me crazy. I despise the woman I'm about to marry and the one I love now despises me. And to top it off I'm going to be a father. This shit just is not right."

"This is why I don't do relationships." Lawrence interjected.

"Yeah okay, so what do you call what you have with Tara?" Adam responded. Lawrence glared at Adam but did not respond.

"So what happened with Stephanie?" Marco inquired. Ivan explained the decision he made to honor his mother's wishes. "I know I have no right to be jealous, but when I saw her at the restaurant with another man I was blinded with anger. I just wanted to rip his fucking head off. I still want to believe that she's mine, she belongs to me. I was her first and I was supposed to be her last. This entire situation is fucked
up."

"Are you saying she was a virgin before you?" Lawrence asked.

He lowered his head as he drained another drink. They all drained their glasses on that information. "You've made your choice so you have to let her go so she can move on with her life." Adam added as he signaled the waiter for another round of drinks.

"First, the decision was made for me and second I don't know how to leave her alone. Did you see how good she looked?" He said to no one in particular. "Enough Ivan regardless of reason, you made your decision. You now need to man up, stop fantasizing about what could have been and start preparing yourself to be a husband and a father." Adam stated firmly.

"Yeah well, fuck you too Adam." Ivan said while signaling for another drink.

CHAPTER FOURTEEN

Stephanie and Mark ended up at her apartment. They sat on the sofa and ate their dinner. Mark started talking about the night she left him.

"Steph I really need you to understand what was going on in my life when we were together. I am not making excuses, but I was a different person back then. As you know my career was just taking off and I thought I had the world by the balls. I had women throwing themselves at me left and right, but I loved you. In my warped twisted thinking I justified my sleeping with other woman by rationalizing that I wanted to wait until our wedding night to make love and it was okay to sleep with other women. I told myself when we did get married I would then be faithful. I thought it would be out of my system and I would eventually marry the woman of my dreams."

Stephanie looked at him with a raised brow as she put her food container on the coffee table. "You know that's bullshit right. You may have had women throwing it at you but you didn't have to take it."

"I know that now Steph but at the time I thought I could have it all. It wasn't until I saw you standing there in that beautiful black sexy lace bra and thong under your coat, it was at that very moment that I realized   that I could have had it all with you if I had just been patient. That was a turning point in my life. I decided I would make myself worthy of you again, but as time went on and you changed your number and moved, short of hiring a private investigator, I thought you were lost to me forever. Then I saw you in the restaurant the other day and I said to myself, God does answer prayers."

"Oh Please, you did not pray to find me." She said laughing "You laugh but I'm serious. I just wanted to get the opportunity to say I'm sorry. I'm sorry for hurting you, for breaking your heart and trust. I am not asking for a second chance just your forgiveness."

She looked into his eyes and saw the sincerity. "I forgive you Mark."

"Good." He said and kissed her on her cheek. He placed his container on the coffee table. "Now you want to tell me about the crazy Italian and why you have not told him you are having his babies?"

"It's complicated."

"I've got time." He said with a smile.

"Well, I use to work for Ivan he was actually my boss."
"Oh an office affair." He said and smiled.

"Something like that. We were instantly attracted to each other, well I was attracted to him it wasn't until later that he confessed that he was also attracted to me. We dated for about a month before our relationship became intimate." *'Maybe less.'* She thought.

"Ouch, you make a brother wait over six months but the white boy only had to wait one month, not fair." He teased.

"You had your chance, you blew it. Anyway. Our relationship was going well until we attended a formal gala and his ex shows up claiming to be pregnant with his baby."

"I don't understand were you sleeping with him without protection?"

"No, we used condoms every time. Here's the crazy part, he told me that he never slept with his ex without using a condom."

"Well either someone's lying or he had a faulty box of condoms. What type were they anyway so I know never to go near them." Mark smirked.

"Whatever, all I know is, I now need to figure out how to handle this situation going forward."

"When are you going to tell him about the babies?"

"I don't know, there is a part of me that doesn't want to tell him. He's starting a new life with his new fiancée and this would just complicate the situation. He chose her over me so I don't want him to feel obligated because of my babies."

"That's bullshit Stephanie, you did not make those babies by yourself and he is obligated and he needs to take responsibility for his actions. Steph don't be one of those women who deny a man the opportunity to be a part of their child's life. I can help in any way you need me to that is until I move."

"You're moving?"

"Yes, I received an incredible job offer from The Jade Corporation. They offered me a shit load of money plus moving expenses to relocate and run their Architect design department in Miami."

"That sounds exciting Mark, congratulations."

"Thanks it's been a long time coming, so what about you, what do you plan to do?"

"I am currently weighing my options. I am thinking about moving to Florida to be with my parents, but I'm not sure."
"If you do, we will be closer together and maybe we can at least mend our friendship. One of the things I loved and missed about our relationship was the long talks we used to have and while I did not expect you to stay a virgin forever, I selflessly hoped that your first experience would have been with me."

She just stared at him. "I know, I know, I ruined that opportunity." He looked at her with sadness in his eyes. "Well I better get going. Steph I would like to continue to see you before I leave, if it's okay. I miss my friend." She nodded as her eyes started to tear up. "Hey, what's wrong?" He said as he hugged her. She loved the feel of him. His masculine smell took over her senses as she leaned into his hug.

"Nothing, my hormones are out of control, but yes I would like to see you again. Thanks Mark I really needed a friend tonight, thanks for being there for me." She walked him to the door and he kissed her on her forehead.

"I'll call you tomorrow."

Ivan was restless as he tossed and turned in his bed before he eventually got up and headed to his exercise room. He needed to work off some energy and the alcohol left in his system. His mind kept going back to Stephanie and her date at the restaurant. He knew he needed to let her go but he loved her and the thought of another man in her bed infuriated him. After a brutal hour of working out he headed to the shower. Ivan got dressed and decided he needed to talk to Stephanie. He grabbed his phone and headed out the door. Once out the door and into a waiting car, his phone rang, He looked at the caller id and cursed.

"What is it?"

"Good morning to you too. I need to talk to you."

"About what."

"About what? Ivan we are going to be married in two months and we need to talk about the ceremony and our living arrangement. We need to talk about purchasing a house. I spoke with my doctor and she believes that I should not be living alone because of the complications I've been having. So I thought we could look at houses and decide on something that would suit us and our baby because we can't live in your condo it is not baby friendly." Ivan was partly listening to Ashley's ranting. He thought about Stephanie, he really needed to let her go this was his fate now. "Alright enough we will start to look for a place next week." He heard her squeal and he held the phone from his ear. "I have to go Ashley."

"Wait Ivan, what about me moving into the condo until we buy a house?" Ashley whined.

"Fine I will make the necessary arrangements, goodbye Ashley." He hung up the phone while she was still talking.

Over the next couple of weeks Mark and Stephanie spent a lot of time together. Stephanie could not believe how much difference a month made. Her stomach felt like it doubled in size and she was wearing her maternity clothes. Mark was fascinated with Stephanie's pregnancy and how much weight she had gained. He thought it was the most beautiful thing in the world. He secretly wished she were carrying his babies. Stephanie enjoyed his company and he enjoyed having his friend back. She helped him with his packing and he was very attentive to her and even planned to attend her next doctor's appointment. They finished the last of wrapping his artwork and pictures. "You know the moving company would have done this." Stephanie said teasingly.

"I know but I didn't want to trust some random person with my stuff that I really care about." The last picture was of the two of them at a formal event.

"We really made a cute couple." Stephanie said as she looked at the picture and smiled.

"Yeah until some jerk screwed everything up." He gave her a smile. "What time is your appointment tomorrow?"

"It's at ten o'clock but if you are busy you don't have to go."

"Are you kidding I wouldn't miss it for the world. I still can't get over the fact that my Steph is having a baby correction babies."

"Well I can believe it because it would have to be babies that would cause me to gain so much weight."

"What are you talking about, you only gained a little and you have filled out in all the right places."

She tossed a pillow from the sofa at him. "So when are the movers coming to get your furniture?" Stephanie asked.

"The early part of next week and I move for good the week after next." Stephanie felt a sudden sense of loss. "I'm going to miss you Mark." Mark sat on the sofa beside her.

"I'm going to miss you too but we will talk on the phone and you will have to come visit me while you still can."

"I know." Stephanie yawned.

"Come here." Mark said to Stephanie and she complied. "Lay down and I can rub your back." Stephanie laid her head in Mark's lap and he rubbed her head, neck, and back. "That feels so good." Stephanie said while yawning. Within minutes Stephanie was sound asleep. Mark gently picked her up and she instinctively put her arms around his neck. He took her to his bedroom and laid her down on the bed. He removed her shoes and pulled the covers over her. He grabbed a pair of pajama pants and headed to the bathroom to shower. Several minutes later he returned to find her still sleeping. He climb in the bed wrapped his arm around her protruding stomach and tried to get some sleep.

A few hours later Stephanie woke up disoriented. *'Where the hell am I?'* She felt an arm around her mid section and turned over to see a sleeping Mark. "What the hell?" She instantly looked under the covers to make sure they both had clothes on.
"You okay?" Mark said half asleep.

"Why am I in your bed Mark?"

"You fell asleep, you were tired and I didn't want to wake you. Is everything ok, are you angry?"

"No next time wake me up and ask."

"I'm sorry. Do you want me to take you home?" He asked as he slowly swung his legs so that his feet were planted on the floor.

"No, go back to sleep, I always wake up in the middle of the night to go to the bathroom, thanks to my two little bundles of joy. Do you have something I can sleep in that's a little more comfortable?"

"Look in the second drawer there are t-shirts and shorts help yourself."
She grabbed a white tee and drawstring shorts both of which were a little too big but it would be comfortable on her big belly.

"Do you have an extra toothbrush?"

"In the medicine cabinet." He said before dozing back to sleep. After exiting the bathroom she thought about going into the guest room but decided against it and climbed back in bed beside Mark. He made her feel secure. Once she settled back into bed, Mark's arm came around her waist again she did not protest.

She just settled in and went back to sleep.

DECEMBER 6th

Mark and Stephanie woke up the next day and there was no awkwardness. They made the bed together, ate breakfast and he took her home to change for her doctor's appointment. Mark was in awe when he heard the babies' hearts beating in unison. The doctor told her she was progressing nicely and scheduled her next appointment. As they were leaving Ashley spotted Stephanie and turned her head so that she would not see her. Ashley heard the gentleman with her say "I can't believe you are almost six months," Stephanie smiled and said "yeah but I look like I'm nine
Months". "You look beautiful Steph." They walked out the door.

Ashley couldn't believe Ivan was going to be late again for her appointment. She had her back to the reception area when she saw Stephanie coming from the back. *'What's she doing here?'* She overheard the handsome black man with her mention that he could not believe she was almost six months. 'six months; Oh My God it can't be. I can't believe that Bitch is pregnant.' She started to feel her heart race. She thought about all the condoms she left behind in Ivan's condo. I can't believe she is pregnant by Ivan. She had to sit down she was feeling light headed. Her name was called and it took a few seconds for it to register. She needed to think fast on how she was going to take care of this problem. She walked back to the examination room. After her appointment, Ashley went home and hoped her plan to get rid of Stephanie would work.

She loved living with Ivan even though they were sleeping in separate bedrooms, but that was only temporary. Eventually he would be back in her bed. When Ivan arrived home he did the usual walk to the bar and made a drink. He did not acknowledge Ashley sitting   in   the   living room. "You missed another appointment." She said disappointed.

"It couldn't be helped I had a meeting."

"Eventually you are going to have to talk to me. We are having a baby and I don't want our baby to feel this hostility."

"I am not in the mood for this conversation. I have work to do I will be in my office."

"I saw Stephanie today at my doctor's office." Ivan stopped in his tracks.

"I overheard her talking to a really handsome man about starting a family. I think they just found out they were having a baby. She's just 5 weeks five weeks but they looked so happy." Ivan never turned around he continued to walk to his office and slammed the door.

I don't believe it. I can't believe she would sleep with someone so soon after our breakup. He sat in his chair leaned his elbows on the desk and dropped his head in his hands and rubbed his eyes. He then laid his head back on the headrest of his chair and closed his eyes. He still remembered her wonderful scent. He picked up the phone and dialed Stephanie's number.

"Hello." Stephanie said softly.

"So I hear congratulations are in order." She could hear the harshness in his voice.

"Ivan, how are you?" She said nervously needing to tell him about the babies.

"I wanted to call and tell you."

"Did you Steph and what were you going to tell me, that you could not keep your God damn legs closed." He yelled.

"What?" Stephanie gasped and Ivan continued his tirade.

"We were only broken up a couple of months and you were already fucking someone else. Were you even a virgin or was that part of your bullshit lies."
He knew she was a virgin when they first made love but he was hurting and he wanted to hurt her. He continued. "So what did you do Stephanie, screw the first man who brought you dinner? You just couldn't wait to fuck your new friend could you? You were over me so fast that you can just gave it up."

"You are a bastard Ivan." Her voice was shaking and she felt nauseous. *'How could he believe I would sleep with someone else so soon?'* "I don't know where you are getting your information but...."
She was crying hysterically. Ivan interrupted her before she could finish he did not want to hear an explanation.

"Just fucking tell me - are you pregnant?" He yelled in the phone.

"Yes, but..."
He interrupted her again he was furious. "Fuck you Stephanie, I'm sorry I ever got involved with you. Have a good life."

He slammed down the phone. His chest tightened he couldn't breathe. He loosened his tie in hopes of getting more air into his lungs, but it didn't work. He closed his eyes and laid his head back so that he could regulate his breathing.

Stephanie hung up the phone, shaking and crying uncontrollably. "What's wrong Steph?" Mark asked really concerned. She was too shaken up to explain right away.
"You need to calm down Stephanie, breathe baby you are going to make yourself sick. Who was that on the phone?"
She couldn't answer her breathing was erratic.

"I'm calling the doctors."

"No, I...I'm fine." She choked out between sobs.

216

"Who was that?"

"It was Ivan. He knows I'm pregnant but he thinks I'm pregnant by you and he would not let me explain. I have never heard him talk to me like that. He came just short of calling me a whore." She grabbed her stomach and started crying again. Mark sat beside her on the sofa and pulled her into his lap. He cradled her and rubbed her back until she calmed down. Mark was so angry He wanted to find Ivan and beat his ass. *'He doesn't deserve her.'* He thought. "Shhh..... just relax." He rocked her while rubbing her back until her breathing was under control. Mark kissed her forehead. "You okay?"

She responded "No, but I will be." She got up. "I need go to the bathroom."

Ashley couldn't take it any longer. *'Did he believe me?'* She walked to his office door and tried to hear if he was on the phone. She quietly opened the door. She saw him sitting in the chair with his head back. Was he crying? Ashley was shocked. In all the time that she had known him she couldn't ever remember him crying. She didn't think he was capable of such emotion. *'Over that bitch, he is crying for that whore.'* She was fuming.

He picked his head up and dialed the phone again. He dialed his brother's number. "I need to talk to you" "Ok." ..."I'm on my way."

'Who was he talking to? Was that Stephanie? Why was he so calm?' Panic sat in her body, she was momentarily immobile. *'What's going to happen when he sees her and she is already showing? He will know that Stephanie is carrying his baby.'* She regained her sense of awareness, stepped away from the door, and went to her room. What was she going to do? She needed to stop him. Just then she heard the front door close. "Shit," she dressed quickly and dialed Stephanie's number. Maybe if she told her Ivan was on his way over she could warn her so she would not open the door. A male voice answered the phone.

"Hello," he said and hoped it was Ivan calling back.

"Hello, you don't know me but I am Ivan's fiancée and he is on his way to see Stephanie. I know he is really angry and it would be best if you made sure he didn't see her because I don't know what he would do."
"If he does come here, I can guarantee you his ass will be leaving in an ambulance, so lady I would advise you to tell him not to make that trip because if he comes near Stephanie I will fuck him up!" Mark slammed down the phone and tried to console Stephanie.

Ivan arrived at his bother house. Adam opened the door with a drink ready for Ivan in his hand. He grabbed the glass and sat on the sofa. They sat in silence for ten minutes. Adam knew when his brother was ready to talk, he would.

"She's pregnant." Ivan said as he gulped his drink. Adam looked at his brother confused.

218

"I know she's pregnant that's why you are in this mess."

"No not Ashley, Stephanie, Stephanie is pregnant." Adam looked at him totally stunned.

"You are having another child?" Adam said confused.

"No, she's not pregnant by me she's pregnant by the clown we saw her with in the restaurant."

"What are you talking about? You guys just broke up."

"That was my thought exactly." Ivan said as he drained his glass and walked over to the bar to pour another drink. "But I guess Stephanie got over me faster than I thought." He said and sipped his new drink and settled back down on the sofa.
"I am such a fool. I can't believe I fell in love with that whore. I can't believe she fucked someone so fast. Why would she do that to us, to herself?" Ivan heard the hurtful words coming out of his mouth but he also knew he still loved her. Adam could not believe the hateful things his brother was saying about Stephanie nor could he believe what he was hearing about Stephanie.

"Are you sure?"

"Yes I called her and she did not deny it." Something didn't sound right to Adam.

"How did you find out?"

"As it turned out, Ashley and Stephanie go to the same doctor. Talk about a fucking coincidence." Adam did not comment but something did not sound right about this story, he kept his comments to himself until he could prove differently. Ivan sat and talked to his brother for a while before heading home.

Ashley sped off heading to Stephanie's home. She had driven by their many times in the past to see Ivan's car sitting outside. She needed to catch him before he confronted Stephanie. *'I will not allow that whore to ruin what I have with Ivan.'*
She loved Ivan and Ivan loved her. Stephanie was not going to come between them.
Ashley was so preoccupied with getting to Ivan that she drove through the red light and a SUV slammed into the driver's side of her car. It spun around and slammed into a street light. Everything happened in slow motion for Ashley. She saw the SUV heading towards her but she could not stop it, the last thing   she remembered was the impact of the other vehicle and the warm and wet feeling just before she was surrounded in darkness.

CHAPTER FIFTEEN

Ivan left Adam's home and decided he needed to see Stephanie. He just needed to see her, to hear her say that she did not love him anymore. He really just wanted to hold her and apologize for what he said. God he still loved her so much so that it hurt. 'I will just talk to her again, I want her to tell me to my face that she moved on and that she is truly happy with her new man.' He arrived at the door and knocked. After a few seconds Mark answered the door and Ivan's mood instantly changed.
"What the fuck do you want? Haven't you upset her enough?" Mark spat.
Ivan got in his face.

"I want to see Stephanie." "Stephanie." Ivan yelled. "I need to see you now."

Mark pushed Ivan away from the door. "What the fuck is your problem? It's out of respect for Steph that I don't whoop your ass right now."

"I would love to see you try." Ivan said and looked into Mark's eyes each man refused to back down both had fire in their eyes. Mark stepped back inside the doorway and slammed it in Ivan's face. Ivan banged on the door and yelled Stephanie's name when her neighbors started opening their doors he looked around and realized he was making a fool out of himself.

"What the hell is wrong with me? Get it together Ivan." He said to himself and ran his hand through his hair. 'Walk *away Ivan, just walked away.'* Once Ivan reached his car his phone rang and he grabbed it and hoped it was Stephanie but it was a number he did not recognize. "Hello." Ivan said harshly. "Hello I'm looking for a Mr. Quinn." "This is he." "Mr. Quinn my name is Dr. Wright, I am calling from Franklin Memorial Hospital, Ms. Ashley Ross was brought in by ambulance and she was unconscious. She has you listed as the contact person; we need you to come in...." Ivan could not hear anything else the doctor was saying. *'What was he talking about Ashley was home in bed.'* His brain was fuzzy and he could hear the person on the phone calling his name. "Mr. Quinn, Mr. Quinn." "Yes I'm on my way." He hung up the phone and immediately dialed his brother. He arrived at the hospital and questioned the nurse at the emergency desk; the doctor came out and escorted him to the back of the emergency room. He was explaining that there was a car accident and Ashley had lost a lot of blood and they needed to operate and the baby had to be delivered.

"Wait what are you talking about it's too soon to deliver the baby." Ivan said stunned this entire ordeal was so surreal. "Ms. Ross suffered a placental abruption." The doctor continued to explain but Ivan was having a hard time comprehending what the doctor was saying.

"Is my baby alive?" He asked the doctor.

Stephanie took a long hot bath and enjoyed the smell of lavender as she listened to her favorite music on her IPod. At some point she dozed off and she could hear knocking at the bathroom door. "Steph are you alright? You've been in there almost an hour." She yelled back that she was fine and would be out in a few minutes. Stephanie struggled to get out of the tub she contemplated getting Mark to help her but decided against it. She finally lifted herself out of the tub, towel dried, and moisturized her body before putting on her pajamas. She exited the bathroom feeling refreshed.

"Steph we need to talk." Mark said as she came into the living room.

"What's up?" She said feeling better after her confrontation with Ivan on the phone.

"You had a visitor while you were in the tub. Ivan came by shouting and demanding to see you. I told him to leave."

Stephanie did not respond immediately. She really did not know how to feel. Instantly she felt anger towards Mark for sending Ivan away, she felt anger towards Ivan for leaving her and treating her like shit. She still loved Ivan so much that it hurt to think about him, and she loved Mark for being her protector. This pregnancy had her emotions all over the place.

Breaking the silence, Mark spoke. "You don't need that kind of stress Steph, it's not good for the babies." Moving the conversation in a slightly different direction. Mark continued. "Have you thought about what you are going to do when your due date is close?" Stephanie gave Mark a confused look.

"Not really, I thought about moving back in with my parents but I was hoping that would be my last option."

"I have an idea." Mark said. "And please think about it before you give me an answer." Stephanie looked at him with a raised eyebrow. "Just hear me out." Mark pleaded with her. "Why don't you come and live with me?"

"No. No. Mark that would not...."

He cut her off before she could finish. "Look, you will be closer to your parents, but not having to actually move in with them. I have more than enough room for you and the babies, if you decided to stay after they are born. Let me take care of you for a while."

"I can't do that Mark. This is not your responsibility and I won't burden you with it."
"It's not a burden, I actually like the idea of helping you through this. It will give me a chance to atone for the hurt I caused you."

"Your apology was enough. Thank you for the offer, I love you for that, but this is a situation that I have to work out with Ivan."

"Steph..." She cut him off

"No, but thank you for the offer." She walked over and kissed him on the cheek.
"Now, let's see what we can find for a late night snack before you head home." Stephanie said making it clear that he was not staying the night. Mark went home and Stephanie settled in bed but could not go to sleep. She

thought about Ivan coming to her home earlier. Maybe he was ready to hear her out. She looked at the clock, it was eleven o'clock. I'm sure he's still awake, maybe I should call him. She picked up her cell phone and dialed his number. His phone went straight to voice mail.

"Hi Ivan, Mark told me you came by, call me I would like to explain everything to you. Okay, bye." She hung up the phone and said, "I love you" softly.

-

After Ashley came out of surgery, Ivan and Samantha waited in the recovery room to see her. The doctor informed them that the surgery was successful and they were able to control the bleeding. The next forty- eight hours would be tricky for both Ashley and the baby and if they pulled through their chances of a full recovery would greatly improve. Ivan called his family to let them know about the baby and Ashley. Ivan's mom wanted to come and help out but Ivan told her not to come, he said he would keep her informed. Ivan spent the next several days at the hospital. He had Betty bring him files to work on and had her retrieve the messages from his phone. Betty came by the hospital daily to deliver Ivan's files and his messages.

He quickly shuffled through the messages and weeded out the ones that he had to return right away when he came across Stephanie's message. She called him the day of the accident, the day he showed up at her apartment and was greeted by her new boyfriend. He balled the message up and decided against throwing it away instead he stuck it in his pocket. Later that evening he called Stephanie. She answered after two rings.

"Hello." She said softly.

"Hello Stephanie." Ivan said coldly. "How are you Ivan?"

"I'm fine."

There was awkward silence.
"I miss you." She said softly wanting him to know how she felt.

"Yeah well it didn't take you long to get over me. I'm returning your call and I don't have much time so what did you want?"

"I wanted to talk to you about my pregnancy. I think you got the wrong impression."

"Look Stephanie I don't have time to listen to your explanation about your pregnancy that is not my concern. I have more pressing things to deal with, take care of yourself. Goodbye Stephanie."

"I still love you." She said just above a whisper.

He felt a pang in his chest. He wanted to yell that he loved her too, but he couldn't.

"Yeah well sometimes love can be delusional." He hung up the phone and returned to Ashley's room.

Stephanie met the girls at Sonny's Restaurant. It felt like forever since the last time they went out together. "Look at you Steph, I can't believe how much weight you gained. Those babies are growing leaps and bounds, but you are glowing baby girl, motherhood is agreeing with you. How do you feel?" Tara asked. "I'm feeling pretty good considering I look like I'm carrying four babies instead of two."

They ordered their food and Brianna turned to Stephanie.

"So have you talked to Ivan? Does he know about the twins?"

"No, I tried to talk to him and he freaked out on me and accused me of whoring around and getting pregnant by Mark. Even after I let him calm down and tried to explain again he went on his rant again. You know what, I'm tired of trying to kiss Ivan's ass to accept my babies. He is the one who chose her over me, he chose her, so as far as I'm concerned I don't owe him a goddamn thing, let alone an explanation of my pregnancy. He should know after everything we've been through that I would not sleep with someone so soon after breaking up with him, let alone get pregnant by someone else."

"Steph, he still needs to know about the babies."

"Look, that's my decision, not yours and I say fuck him. He left me; he hurt me, just walked away like I meant nothing to him after I gave him everything. He is choosing to marry her because she is pregnant." A single tear rolled down her cheek. "I loved him so much and he just kept stomping on my heart. I can't keep being his doormat and I definitely don't want him back in my life out of obligation."

"Alright Steph, don't get upset, it's your decision and we'll support you on whatever you decide." Tara said and tried to sooth her.

"Good, because I decided to move to Miami with Mark until the babies are born."

"WHAT?" Brianna and Tara said in unison.

"Awh hell no, I will support you in everything but that. Has this pregnancy caused you to lose your mind?" Tara said angrily.

"Stephanie you can't do this, you need to think this through. Don't you remember how bad he hurt you? Think Steph, you are leaving one heartache for another, stay here with us, we will make sure that you are taken care of." Brianna pleaded with her.
You know we've got your back in anything that you need. You can move in with me, I have more than enough room." Brianna said.

"I can't impose on you like that." Stephanie said.

"But you can impose on that bastard that broke your heart. Do you remember the bad shape you were in when you found out he was cheating on you? We sure as hell do. He screwed you over and never looked back. Don't do this to yourself baby girl you are just setting yourself up for more hurt." Tara said.

"I appreciate what you guys are saying but I don't have feelings for Mark like that anymore, we are friends and he extended the invitation as friends and nothing more." Stephanie did not want to go into how Mark said this would give him a chance to make up for the hurt he caused her because they would just twist his words into some ulterior motive, "In the end, it's my decision and I have given it serious consideration. I don't think I can stay in town while he marries her and gives her the life I thought we would have together."

"You are treading in dangerous territory Steph, seriously think about this before you go down that road. When Ivan finds out about his babies, and oh.... trust me, he will find out, there is going to be a major fall out that will destroy whatever's left of your relationship with him." Brianna said.

"He already destroyed our relationship when he said goodbye." Their food arrived and they ate in silence. As they were leaving the restaurant Stephanie turned to her friends.

"I love you guys and I will think about it and let you guys know what I decide."

Stephanie went home, took a shower, laid down and tried to weigh all her options. Financially she would be okay until the babies were born, but she would need help for the first couple of months. 'I can't stay here and be constantly reminded of his decision.' Stephanie dozed after making a decision.

"Hey Mark, how's the moving going?" Stephanie asked after she called him the next morning.

"Done. Actually I just completed settlement on my house and I'm flying out to Miami next week." There were a few seconds of silence. "Is everything okay Steph?"

"Yes, I was just wondering if your offer is still open."

"Of course it is, did you make a decision?"

"I did. Do you have time this evening to come over so we can talk about it, I will make you dinner."

"Don't bother because if you are considering coming with me, I will bring dinner over to celebrate."

"How about you bring dessert I will cook and after we can talk. You can decide if you want to celebrate."

Mark came over at six o'clock and dinner was ready. After dinner and dessert Stephanie and Mark sat on the sofa to discuss Stephanie's decision.

"First, I just want to thank you again for the offer to stay with you."

"This doesn't sound like the response I was hoping for." Mark said suspiciously.

"Hear me out, like I said I want to thank you for the offer, but I need to know something?"

"What is it?"

"I don't understand why you are willing to take on another man's responsibility." She said and looked him directly in his eyes for any hints of deceitfulness.

"Well if you are asking me what my intentions are towards you, I would have to say that I love and care about you. I get that you are still in love with your babies' father and I can accept that. I want to do this for you. He said earnestly. "You can't even imagine how I struggled with not having you in my life when you left, I wanted to make it right and even if we never get together again I can move on knowing I did right by you."

"Thank you for saying that. I would like to take you up on your offer, but we have to set ground rules. First, you need to know why I came to this decision. Both Bri and Ty offered for me to move in with them, when it was close to my due date, but I can't bear to live in the same city with Ivan and his soon to be wife and their new baby. He thinks I'm pregnant by you, and I am still so angry with him for thinking that I would jump into bed with someone else so soon after our breakup. I am not ready to tell him about the babies yet, if ever."

Mark interrupted her. "For the record, I think that's a bad idea Steph. As much as I don't like the man he has a right to know about his babies and...." Stephanie put her hand up to stop him.

"It's my decision and I will decide if and when I tell him."

Mark continued. "Okay, but I think you're wrong."
"

Whatever." Stephanie said harshly. "Anyway, if I move in with you it will be like having a roommate, you have to let me pull my weight financially." Mark started to protest and she interrupted. "Mark, that is the only way I will agree to this arrangement, otherwise I will have to move in with my parents." She winced at that thought.

"Go on." Mark said irritated.

"I don't want to be more of a burden than I'm already going to be, so you have to promise me that if there is someone you are interested in dating that you will pursue it. I couldn't bear staying with you knowing that I am putting a cramp in your love life." Mark stared at Stephanie, but did not respond.

"Lastly, I don't want you to feel obligated to get involved with the babies.

You don't have to attend their doctor's appointments or be there for the birth. I'm sure my mom, my sister, Bri and Ty will be there. I want me moving in with you to be as least disruptive as possible for your life." Mark looked into her eyes, but did not speak right away. He moved closer to Stephanie on the sofa, and put his arm around her shoulder.

"When I asked you to move in with me, I was fully aware of what I was asking. I intend to be there for you every step of the way with your pregnancy.
I intend to go to every appointment, help you through all your aches and pains, and if you will have me I would be honored to be there in the delivery room.

I am in this with you for the long haul. You need to know this before we move together; I am not your roomy. I am someone who loves and cares about your well-being and will help you through this difficult time in your life." Mark turned his body towards her palming her face with his hands. "Stephanie, look at me."
She lifted her eyes to meet his gaze.
"I am not asking you to fall in love with me again. I acknowledge that I blew that opportunity, but let me take care of you, even if it's only for a few months." Stephanie could see the sincerity in his eyes. She kissed him on the cheek and thanked him. He noticed a tear rolling down her cheek. Mark placed his lips softly on her eyelids and trailed kisses down her cheeks until he reached her lips.

He kissed her continuously giving her light pecks on her soft lips. Finally, he brought his lips on hers firmer rubbing his tongue along her bottom lip encouraging her to open. Reluctantly, she did, and he used the opportunity to take her tongue into his mouth and sucked on it feverously. Stephanie closed her eyes taking in and enjoying the intimacy. God she missed this, she missed Ivan. The thought of Ivan caused her to pull back, feeling such a sense of guilt. Mark placed his forehead on her forehead.

"I'm sorry."

"Its fine, but you have to know that I still love Ivan and if you can't handle that, I can't move in with you."

"Okay Steph, I will never pressure you, but know that I still love you, and that has never stopped. I only ask if your feelings start to change that you won't fight them."

She nodded. "Then we're good." He pulled Stephanie into an embrace. Her mind reeled from everything going on in her life, but she knew she needed to move on. Ivan did not want her. She needed to realize that as she was entering a new chapter living in a new city and preparing to be a new mom. She rubbed her stomach and smiled. Mark placed his hand over hers as they rubbed in unison. Mark felt her hand slowly fall away as he continued to caress her belly. He heard a soft snore and realized she was sleep. He looked at her while she slept. *'You are so beautiful. I will show you how much I love you and deserve a second chance.'* This was his opportunity to show her how good they could be together. He already loved the babies she was carrying and if given the opportunity would make her a great husband and father to her babies. Mark stood, scooped Stephanie in his arms and carried her to the bedroom. In a couple of days they would be in their new house, and with any luck, ready to start a new life with the woman he loved.

ABOUT THE AUTHOR

Sage Young is a writer of erotically sensual novels. Currently residing in Philadelphia, PA she is entering the literary arena this summer with her debut novel, "DELUSIONAL LOVE". Sage is an avid reader of all things, but erotic romance novels in particular.

Sage uses every spare moment to indulge in her second favorite passion, writing. Her favorite saying is, "Always Explore the Possibilities". She hopes that you will enjoy her novel and looks forward to your feedback.

COMING THE WINTER OF 2013

THE SAGA CONTINUES

DEFINED LOVE

Prologue

'How did my life get here?' Thought Ivan Quinn, founder and CEO of The Quinn Corporation. Handling the day-to-day operations of a billion dollar company was not difficult for him but dealing with all the drama in his personal life was taking its toll.

Ivan sat in the living room of his condominium, in the dark and nursed another drink. He reached into his pocket and pulled out a picture of his beautiful baby girl Angel.

He kissed the picture as he closed his eyes and thought of happier times, a time when his life was not so complicated. He had Stephanie, the love of his life by his side his business was expanding and he was happy, truly happy. Then the bottom fell from under him. He was now engaged to Ashley Ross who was the mother of his child.

Ivan did not love Ashley, in fact he despised her, but he made a promise to his mother. The hospital had to deliver his beautiful baby girl, but Ashley remained in a coma since the car accident.

Stephanie Young, the love of his life was pregnant by another man and had moved to Florida with him. Could my life get any worse? He thought as he continued to nurse his drink, knowing that he would soon have to return to the hospital where he spent most of his time, at Ashley's bedside, since the accident.

CPSIA information can be obtained at www.ICGtesting.com
Printed in the USA
BVOW04s1837100414

350319BV00011B/237/P